A
KILLING
FREEZE

A KILLING FREEZE

LYNN HALL

MORROW JUNIOR BOOKS
NEW YORK

Printed in the United States of America.

1 2 3 4 5 6 7 8 9 10

Library of Congress Cataloging-in-Publication Data
Hall, Lynn.
A killing freeze.
Summary: High school junior Clarie sees her small
town's winter festival disrupted and her father's
snowmobile business threatened by a set of grisly
multiple murders.
[1. Mystery and detective stories] I. Title.
PZ7.H1458Ki 1988 [Fic] 88-5143
ISBN 0-688-07867-2

A
KILLING
FREEZE

ONE

I still love Harmon Falls, but I'll never feel quite the same about my town after what happened here last week.

Most of my friends can hardly wait to get through the next year and three months, to graduate and go to college or whatever. They seem to feel obligated to sneer at Harmon Falls because it's a little dinky town where nothing ever happens.

I have an advantage over them, though. My dad raised me to think clearly and directly, to look inside myself for answers rather than to follow the crowd. So I've known for years that my life here with Dad, in our funny little house in Harmon Falls, Minnesota, is exactly what I want my life to be.

Dad always says that small towns are microcosms, with all the good and bad of human nature but on a small enough scale that it can be accepted and dealt with, and even understood if you try.

I'm still trying to understand and deal with . . . but I'm starting at the wrong end of the story.

Harmon Falls has a huge annual winterfest the first weekend in February and this year, as usual, Dad was the chairman of the Fest Committee. The Fest lasted four days, Thursday through Sunday, and our school let out Friday because so many of us were involved in it. But the principal let me take off Wednesday and Thursday, too, so I could help Dad.

The Fest had been Dad's idea in the first place, ten years ago. He has a little shop downtown that sells snowmobiles in winter and bikes in summer, so he wanted to promote snowmobile races. The thing grew from just a few events into this four-day giant it is now, with dog-sled races, cross-country ski races, mutt races for the kids, an ice sculpture competition, silly sled races, snowball games, everything. A big chili supper and dance on Saturday night, the works.

It's the high point of the year for Dad and me, even though it means busting our butts chasing details. For instance, I spent all day Wednesday in Dad's shop, which was headquarters for the Fest. I stuck labels on one hundred eighty trophies. I checked the trophies against the master list and ran down the three missing ones that the trophy company sent to the wrong address. I answered at least three million phone calls and sent people out four times to find Dad when emergencies came up.

Dad was running in circles himself. He didn't trust anyone else to lay out the course for the snowmobile races, and while he was doing that, Harvey Peterson came in and told me they were having trouble with the ice mold in Lions Park, across the road from our shop. The ice mold is a huge box, like a coffin for a fat midget, that they fill with water and freeze giant cubes of ice in for the ice sculpture contest. And before Dad could get that straightened out, the guy in charge of the ski races came in with a broken drive belt on the snowmobile that he used to pull the track-laying machine to lay out the ten-kilometer and three-kilometer ski races.

Meanwhile, down at the lake, the two guys

who were supposed to be clearing the snow off the ice for the mutt races were having practically a knock-down, drag-out fight over where to lay the course.

The guy with the concessions truck called and wanted to know where he was going to get the electrical hookup he needed, and I didn't know and didn't care at that point.

Late in the afternoon, the first of the ice sculptors started coming in to sign in and get their block numbers. The blocks of ice, at least the ones that had been finished before the waterline to the mold froze up, were set up in Lions Park with cardboard numbers on them, and each of the nine sculptors on my entry list was assigned a block. But they weren't allowed to start carving till the next morning at nine.

Around five, Dad came in. He and I look just alike. We're both tall and skinny, with black curly hair and long, pointed noses with red tips. His is usually dripping from the cold. Mine doesn't drip. That's how you can tell us apart. Well, also I'm a girl, but you'd have to look close to be sure of that. I am, shall we say, in no danger of tipping over frontward from the weight of my figure. But that's okay. Dad and I wear each other's clothes a lot, and it's handy, especially since neither one of us is good at remembering to do laundry.

There is no Mom in the picture, obviously. I'm

what is quaintly known as a bastard. Luckily, nobody in Harmon Falls gives a hoot. Dad got this girl pregnant when they were both in high school. She hated the whole idea, was terrified about giving birth, refused to get married even though Dad wanted to. I was born seven weeks premature, and while I was still in an incubator in the hospital, she took off running, and not even her parents knew where she was for four years.

So there was Dad, seventeen years old and still in high school, with a tiny preemie baby on his hands. Everybody tried to make him give me up for adoption, but he wanted me, and by God he kept me. He got three jobs, and his mom and dad took care of me, and I'm the greatest thing that ever came into his life. He tells me so—a lot.

He shoved his way through the shop, which was full of stand-arounders—Bernie Rodas and Ray Proctor and Jim Aherns, all sitting around talking about what they were going to do to each other in the snowmobile races. Bernie Rodas is a woman, but she's another one you have to look close at to tell, especially in her snowmobile suit.

The shop was just a little place anyhow, a former gas station on the corner of Cardinal Road and the highway, which is also the main street of town. In what used to be the service bays of the gas station, we've got three Arctic Cat snowmobiles on display, plus two racks of accessories and a bunch of miscellaneous junk. In the main room, which is tiny, there's just Dad's desk and a couple of files, big windows on two sides with benches under them, and a pop machine and a table with coffee stuff on it. You get someone the size of Bernie in her snowmobile suit, plus a couple of other guys, plus the cartons of trophies and all my clipboards with entry lists and time schedules, and you've got a roomful.

Dad edged his way around the desk and messed up my hair. "What's the latest disaster?"

"Did Harvey find you? The waterline to the ice mold froze up, and they've got one more block to do. He was going to try to melt it down with an acetylene torch if he could find one. He figures it'll take a good ten hours to freeze the block all the way through."

Dad nodded and wiped his nose on his jacket cuff. "He found me. What else?"

"The trophy company sent the three ski trophies to the wrong address but they promised they'd get over here with them by tomorrow morning or die trying."

"That seems only fair. Anything else?"

I sighed. "Some woman wanted to know if she could trade kids. Her daughter is entered in the mutt race, but has a conflict Saturday morning with a piano recital, so could the younger brother drive the dog in the race instead? I told her yes. Okay?"

"Fine. Anything else?"

"They were having trouble with the drive belt for—"

"No sweat. We got that running. That's where I've been. Listen, Clarie, get out of here before they arrest me for child abuse. Go home, feed Rover, feed yourself, bring me back a sandwich or, no, forget it. I'll get somebody to bring me something from the cafe. You stay home and relax. I'll stick around down here till things settle down."

He shoved me out of the chair and sank into it himself, unzipping his jacket and loosening his boot tops. He was the most even-tempered person I knew, totally unflappable, but I could see the strain in his face. This Fest was the biggest thing in his life. He started planning it a full year in advance, and it brought in about half our income for the winter in snowmobile sales and repairs. It was no wonder he looked a little taut the night before the opening day.

"I'll stay and help," I said.

"No, you won't. You'll go home and feed our starving dog, and get yourself an early night. I'll need you even more tomorrow."

I snorted. "Our starving dog has probably already bummed himself three dinners from the neighbors."

But I zipped up my boots and pulled on my parka. I was more than willing to be shoved out of that room and into the winter twilight.

Ray Proctor unbent from where he'd been half-lying on the bench by the window, and said, "I'll run you home, Clarie."

"No, thanks. I need the fresh air and exercise."

Ray Proctor made me uneasy. He was probably harmless, but for the last year or so he'd been trying to get close to me or get me alone, and he was a creep. I'm sorry, but that's the most polite way I can describe him. He was probably mid-twenties, never had jobs for very long, drank a lot, and never had anything nice to say about anyone or anything. He already had the start of a beer belly, and I'd swear he never brushed a tooth in his life. They had kind of a greenish scum on them.

I'd have disliked him only mildly except for something he did last summer. He was working for our neighbor, Mrs. Amling, who was one of my all-time favorite people. She had a little A-frame house in the woods behind our place, and she lived there alone with her dogs and cats and a darling pygmy goat. She was a widow, and she wrote children's books. She was a very quiet person, shy I think, but she had the neatest sense of humor.

She'd hired Ray to cut firewood for her last summer, but after a couple of weeks she fired him and started doing it herself. She told me Ray was a nuisance, always sticking his head into the house and interrupting her when she was writing, so she'd decided she'd rather wrestle with the chain saw herself than have him around.

But the way Ray told it, he quit because Mrs. Amling was making passes at him. I mean, come on. Nobody around town believed it—Mrs. Amling was so nice and Ray was such a barf-bag—but the fact that he would say something like that turned me off completely.

So I walked up Cardinal Road in the winter twilight even though I was pooped from the day's hassles and a ride would have felt good. Still, it was a nice walk. Cardinal wasn't enough of a road to have sidewalks, but it also wasn't enough of a road to have traffic, so I trudged up the car tracks in the middle of the road, pulling on my padded mittens and enjoying the scenery. The houses were scattered and small along here, and set far back from the road among huge, straight-spined white pines. The road climbed for a block, then dipped to wind its way out of town through a wooded valley that followed Fox Creek.

My cheeks reddened to match the tip of my nose before I was halfway up the hill. Over the past weekend we'd had a huge snowfall, almost two feet, which made Dad ecstatic. No worries about not having enough snow for the Fest. But then Monday and Tuesday had been in the forties and sunny, so a lot of that snow compacted down and disappeared. By today, Dad was sweating it, but I could tell the air was sharper now, well down into the twenties, and blowing in from the west were fat, low snow clouds, dark gray with a yellow-green tinge to them.

In fact, the flakes were already starting as I crested the hill and started down into the valley. I tried a few running slides on the packed tire tracks, but I kept hitting gravel, so I quit.

Our house was weird looking. I loved it. Dad and I built it entirely with our own hands, starting when I was about ten. It took a couple of years of working on it weekends before we could move in, but that was okay. We'd been living with Grandma and Grampa since I was born, and they were great, but we wanted our own place, and they wanted to move to Texas for Grampa's asthma. Dad and I could have stayed in their house but it was right on the highway, practically downtown, and our dogs kept getting run over, and besides, Dad and I loved being in the woods.

So Dad bought these three acres on Cardinal Road from a guy he knew who owed him for two snowmobiles he'd bought and wrecked and never paid for. He cut down fourteen big pines right in the middle of the three acres, cut them up into log-lengths and cured them a year. He got some of his buddies to help pour a cement slab and footings around the edge and to rough in the plumbing and wiring. All that took about another year because we didn't have much money.

Then finally we started the walls. That was the most exciting summer I ever had. The pine logs only went up about three feet high, and we didn't want to cut down any more of our trees, so the bottom of the walls are log with cement mortar, and the tops of the walls are scrap lumber Dad and I got from tearing down two old houses in town. He let me help with that because I was twelve by that time. We got wall siding, doors, windows and windowframes, all kinds of neat stuff from those old houses. Then we found a terrific buy on screen doors at a railroad salvage place in Rochester, so we built a screened-in porch around three sides of the house.

It's just a little house, three rooms and a bathroom. The living room and kitchen are all one, across the front, and then we each have a little square room of our own in the back, with the bathroom in between.

We've lived in it three and a half years now, and every year it gets better: tile floors over the cement, then big shaggy rugs over the tile, and a big wood stove in the living room with doors that open so it's like a fireplace. We painted the log part of the inside walls a cream color and stained the planks on the top part of the walls with pine stain. We've got huge tapestries of deer and pheasants and stuff like that hanging all over the walls. They're just cheap ones—we buy them at flea markets in the summer—but I like them.

"Rover," I yelled as I stomped the snow off my boots on the front porch. As usual, he wasn't there. He was a beagle, and the name Rover fit him perfectly. I'd voted against the name when we got him. I said Rover was the commonest dog name in the world. But Dad said no, it isn't. Have you ever actually known a dog named Rover? And I had to admit I knew Tippys and Mistys and Maxes, but no Rovers.

Rover had an excellent doghouse, built by me at great trouble and expense, with foam insulation in the walls and everything, and it sat right on the porch out of the wind. But did he ever stay in it? Was he ever home when we wanted him? Of course not. He was over at Mrs. Amling's, pretending her dogs weren't both spayed. Or begging food from her. Or down at the Thompsons', barking at their cat.

"Come on, you stupid hound," I yelled. I was pooped and starving, and I did not want to have to go looking for Rover before I went in and collapsed.

But I knew it would be even harder to make myself get booted and jacketed up again if I did go in and get warm, so I cussed awhile, tromped around the house once, yelling, then started off down the path behind the house.

Mrs. Amling's house was beyond the curve in Cardinal Road, so the backs of our properties met at right angles back in the woods. We had a little bit of a path, worn at first by Rover in search of food and sex, and me in search of Rover. The path got deeper later, as I started spending more time with Mrs. A. Until she came along I hadn't realized how much I missed having a mom. I'd always figured Dad and my friends were enough for me. But Mrs. Amling was just so special, and she made me feel special because she liked me, maybe loved me a little. I sure loved her, although I was too shy to say so.

Her place, like ours, sat in a small clearing in the pines. It was a good-sized house, for an A-frame. It was just a huge triangle of roof, with no side walls except on the north side where the ground sloped downhill. It had dormers on either side, so it looked like two roofs crisscrossed, with big picture windows on the south and west ends.

Behind it was a shed like a tiny barn, where Gruffy, her pygmy goat, lived.

I stopped to say hi to him, and he stood against his fence to get his head scratched. He was a beautiful blue-gray color with black penciling on his face and white on his legs and chest. He was always wanting his head scratched, but today his climbing and bleating were frantic.

"What's the matter, Gruffy?"

I could see that his feed pan was empty and so was his water bucket. That was unusual.

A dog howled. Chills fingered my spine and touched my scalp. Something was wrong here. I could see Mrs. Amling's car in front of the house where it always was, but there were no lights on inside, and no smoke from the chimney.

"Mrs. Amling?" I yelled. Her dogs began barking frantically, but I couldn't see them. They sounded as if they were outdoors somewhere. I started around the house, following their din.

She was there beside the house, and she was dead.

TWO

She lay facedown, arms upflung, looking grotesquely childlike in her blue coveralls. Against either side of her body, her dogs huddled, shivering and looking up at me.

It was several seconds before disbelief released me. "Mrs. Amling?" I said foolishly as I knelt and put my hand on her shoulder. The stiffness of death was unmistakable, even through the thickly padded coveralls. And there was blood on her scalp and frozen on the ground above her head.

A small paw clawed at my thigh. "I know, Betty," I said in a thin voice. I picked up the little black cocker and grasped the collar of the other dog, a fat old Dalmatian. Domino balked at my pull. I pulled again, then realized that Domino couldn't walk. She was rigid with cold. How long had these dogs been out here, I wondered? Hours? Days?

I carried Betty Cocker into the house by the basement door, which was just a few steps down an embankment from where Mrs. Amling lay. I set the dog on the floor near the furnace, then went back and hefted Domino into my arms and carried her inside.

I was so light-headed when I set her down that I nearly tipped over on top of her. There was a faint ringing in my ears, like the time I'd ripped my hand on a nail when Dad and I were tearing down one of the old houses and I'd nearly passed out from watching myself bleed.

No time for passing out now, and no Dad here to comfort me and make me sit with my head between my knees. I forced my legs to carry me upstairs to the kitchen, where the telephone was.

Who to call? Who to call?

Keith, I decided finally.

"Sheriff's office," the familiar voice answered. "Dittmer speaking."

"Keith, this is Clarie. I'm out at Mrs. Amling's house, and she's dead, I think. She's lying outside, and she looks really . . ." I started choking up then, and couldn't talk.

"You stay there and don't touch a thing, honey. I'll get an ambulance and be right out. Are you okay?"

I nodded, forgetting I was talking on the phone and he couldn't see me. But he was already replaced by a dial tone.

I called Dad. Then, remembering Betty Cocker and Domino, I called the vet's and the office girl said she'd send one of the guys as soon as someone got in from farm calls.

The Sheriff's car pulled in then, with the ambulance right behind it. I went outside and motioned them silently toward Mrs. Amling.

Keith looked like a big blond bear in his tan winter uniform jacket with the earflap-cap. His new beard was coming in red. He and my Dad were buddies from when they were in school, so I'd known Keith forever. He was one of the guys who helped when we were building our house.

Usually he clowned around a lot and teased me, but he was serious now. He bent over the body, waved the ambulance guys away, then walked slowly around, looking at the bare ground, at the blood near the top of her head, at the house and the woods. He circled wider, to where the snow began, and stared at the tracks in it. The ground near the house where Mrs. Amling lay was bare of snow because it sloped to catch the winter sun and because of the heat radiating from the house. Mrs. Amling had planted a border of crocuses next to the house because it was so warm there.

"You go on back in," Keith said to me. "I'll be in in a minute."

Dad drove in then, slammed out of the truck and came to me at a run. "Are you okay?" he asked, grabbing me by the shoulders, hugging me hard.

"Take her in the house, Mel," Keith said. "She doesn't need to be seeing this."

Dad and I went in through the basement door. He flipped on the light switch because it was full twilight by now, and the basement was dim. It was an unfinished-looking room, plywood walls and rough storage shelves, and laundry equipment against the far wall. An old chrome dinette set stood near the clothes dryer. Mrs. Amling used it to fold and sort on. Dad and I pulled out peeling plastic dinette chairs and sat down. Betty Cocker was in my lap instantly, shivering and whining. I wrapped my arms around her.

Domino still sat in the position I'd left her in. She wasn't shivering. Her eyes weren't focusing. While I stared at her, she sank to the floor and stretched out, wheezing loudly and fighting for breath. Dad got down beside her and stroked her, which was about all anybody could do for her at that point.

I told him what little I knew, and I told it again when the ambulance had driven off and Keith had come in.

"I just came over looking for Rover and she was lying there like that. The dogs were about frozen from sitting out there with her, so I brought them in here and called you. She's definitely . . . ?"

Keith nodded, sniffed, sat down on the corner of the table and shook a cigarette out of his pocket. "Hell of a thing," he said. "Nice woman like that."

"What happened?" Dad asked. "Could you figure it out?"

Keith shook his head and blew smoke. "Probably the blow on the head, but I couldn't find anything around there that could have made it. It wasn't a blow with anything blunt, it was more sharp and deep. . . ." He looked at me.

I figured he wanted me to go away so he could talk. It was the kind of look he used to give me when he and Dad got onto the subject of women. But I was damned if I was leaving.

I said, "Could you tell me how long she'd been lying out there?"

"Quite a while. A day or two, anyhow. The autopsy'll pin that down."

A day or two. While I was busy with the Fest, Mrs. A. had been lying out here, dying alone. I couldn't stand it.

Dad said, "You're going to do an autopsy then?"

"Have to if there's any question about cause of death, and there sure is a question here. Lots of questions. You guys knew her. Did she have any enemies, anybody who might have wanted to . . . ?"

I stared at him. It hadn't even occurred to me that someone had done this to Mrs. Amling. Just the fact of her death had been enough for my brain to try to handle.

Dad and I looked at each other and shook our heads. He said, "She was just a nice, quiet person, Keith. I never heard her say a bad word about anybody, well, except Ray Proctor when she fired him last summer. She had him up here cutting firewood for her for a while. I was out back one day and saw her out there by herself, cutting up dead branches with her chain saw. I went over and gave her a hand, and she told me Ray was kind of a nuisance to have around, you know, interrupting her when she was writing, that sort of thing. Well, you remember he was going around town telling it like she'd been making passes at him or some such foolishness. You remember. There wasn't any truth in it, I know her well enough to know that. . . ."

His voice ran down, as the loss of a well-liked neighbor began to sink in.

Keith stared at his cigarette end. "That little bit of dust-up doesn't seem like anything that would bring on . . ." He motioned toward where the body had lain. "Did she have any men friends? Any family around here?"

I spoke up firmly. "She didn't have any men friends. I know. We talked about it. Her husband died years ago, and I asked her one time if she ever went out on dates or anything like that. She just kind of laughed. Said if she ever found another one like her husband she might consider it, but she figured he was one of a kind. We are—we *were*—pretty good friends." I choked up, cleared my throat and went on. "She never talked about men that way, you know, romantically. What she mostly talked about was the book she was working on, or arguments with her editor, or whether to get a nanny goat to keep Gruffy company. Or about her vegetable garden, or whether to build a deck out from her bedroom."

"No family?" Keith asked again.

I shook my head. "I don't think so. I know she never had children. She had something wrong with her tubes or something. And I know both of her parents are dead. She has a sister, out in Colorado somewhere, but they weren't very close."

There was a noticeable silence in the room, beneath our voices. We all turned and looked at Domino. She was no longer wheezing. Or breathing. I joined Dad on the floor beside her and then my control slipped. I bawled into Dad's jacket, so hard he had to sit me on his lap and rock me like a baby. I'd have felt silly if I hadn't been with Dad and Keith.

"I don't know why I'm crying harder for an old dog than for her," I sobbed. "What's the matter with me?"

"That's the way it works," Keith growled softly.

When the vet finally got there, he flipped back Domino's eyelid and shook his head. We told him what had happened.

"Well, if this old girl was sitting outside for very long in this weather with no more coat than she carries, it's a wonder she was still alive when you found her. Let's take a look at Betty."

She was a curly little black cocker, too small for her breed and with a forbidden white patch on her chest. Mrs. Amling had found her at the animal shelter just last year when Domino started showing signs of slowing down.

The vet listened to her lungs while I held her

on my lap. She seemed not to want to let go of me. He rolled back her eyelid and checked her temperature and gave her a shot.

"She's got some congestion in there, but she's young and strong. She should be able to throw it off. Who's going to be taking care of her, now that . . . ?"

Dad and I looked at each other. "Me, I guess," I said.

"Fine. Just keep her inside where it's warm, keep her quiet if you can, and let me know if her breathing starts sounding labored. That's an awful shame about Mrs. Amling. She was a nice lady. I always liked her. What caused it, do you know?" He asked that of Keith.

"It's under investigation," Keith said, standing as though he wanted to look more official.

When the vet left, the three of us unraveled in separate directions. Keith went outside for one more look around by flashlight; Dad, at my suggestion, took water and goat pellets out to Gruffy; and I zipped my parka around Betty's shivering body and started home. The vet had taken Domino along to be disposed of in a manner I didn't want to think about.

Rover was waiting by the door when I got home. He was thrilled to see Betty, but she ignored him and stayed plastered to me. I couldn't get her to eat anything, but she did drink a whole dog-dish full of water. I tried to imagine what she and Domino must have gone through, tried to imagine how much a dog can understand about death. Maybe more than we do, I thought.

When Dad came in, I made us some tomato soup and a pile of peanut-butter and cracker sandwiches. He ate most of it. I just couldn't get interested. The death itself was awful enough to try to absorb, but the possibility that it might have been murder shook my foundations. Death happens in Harmon Falls like anywhere else. Old people pass away in the retirement home. Babies die of birth defects or crib death. Every spring at graduation time, there's a fatal accident in the news, teenagers driving drunk. Those are awful.

But the idea of someone coming into our nice little woodsy neighborhood, on Cardinal Road, in Harmon Falls, Minnesota, and actually committing murder, actually hitting a dear, little, middle-aged lady who wrote children's books, hitting her with something . . . I couldn't think about that. It was obscene.

I expected Dad to go back down to the shop after supper, but he didn't. He sat staring at the television with Rover shoved into the chair beside him. And, for the first time I could remember, he locked the door when we went to bed.

* * *

Dad left for the shop early the next morning, with orders for me to come on down whenever I felt like it. I tried again to get Betty Cocker to eat, but she wouldn't. Maybe her own familiar food, I decided.

I had to go over this morning anyway to get food and water for Gruffy. I wasn't sure what I'd do if the house was locked, because the goat food was in the basement and there was no outside water. But when I got there, Keith's car was parked in front of the house. I went in through the basement and up into the main room.

It was a steep triangle of a room, all window on the far end, with the pale wood ceiling vaulting to a high peak. The side walls were just sloping extensions of the ceiling. The back wall was a huge stone fireplace with a balcony crossing it. There was a tiny bedroom up there, I knew, and a little kitchen tucked behind the fireplace. Even now, with the fireplace dead, it was a cozy, pleasant house, full of bowls of winter-blooming amaryllis and stacks of books and manuscripts. An old brown corduroy sofa stood at a right angle to the hearth, with yellow flowered chairs across from it and a shaggy sheepskin rug between. Along one of the sloping side walls was a mammoth desk with her typewriter and drifts of papers and an electric teapot. She always said she couldn't write without her tea.

My throat lumped up.

"Keith?" I called.

His head appeared over the balcony above me. "Clarie? What are you doing here?"

"I came to feed the goat and get some of her dog food for Betty. Is that okay?"

"Yeah, I guess. I shouldn't let anybody in here till the investigation is complete, but I guess I can trust you not to touch anything."

He lowered his bulk awkwardly down the spiral staircase and stood sweating lightly, looking at me.

"Find anything?" I asked.

He wiped his face on his forearm and said, "Found the sister's phone number, that was the main thing. She's away on a Caribbean cruise. A neighbor who was watering her plants answered the phone. She told me Mrs. Amling's sister would be back on Sunday, but she didn't know what ship she was on. I'll have to call back Sunday, to notify her."

"That must be awful to have to do things like that."

"It ain't the most fun part of the job, kid." He went to the big desk and started to stir cautiously through the papers on it. Most were manuscript pages. A few were pencil-printed letters from children who read her books. She loved getting letters from kids. Lots of times in the early winter twilight, I'd curl up on the brown sofa, close to the fire, and listen while she read me the letters she'd gotten that day from kids who loved her books. And sometimes she talked out her ideas with me for a new book she was working on. She'd told me once that I was the only person she'd trusted to listen to her book ideas since her husband died. That made me feel so great.

"She was starting on a new series of stories," I said. "Something about a family of squirrels. She was all excited about it. She said she was hoping to get some kind of award with it if she could find an illustrator good enough to do the pictures for it."

There was a stack of sealed letter-sized envelopes on the desk, ready to be mailed. I glanced at the top one, then hesitated, and looked at it again. It was addressed to Richard Moline, and the address was in St. Paul. Something familiar about the name snagged my mind.

"I've heard this name just recently," I said, pointing to the envelope but not wanting to touch anything. "It wasn't from Mrs. Amling, but I can't think where . . ."

Keith picked it up, turned it over, then ripped it open. It was neatly typed on Mrs. Amling's stationery. He read it aloud.

"Dear Mr. Moline, I'm sorry to have to be unpleasant about this, but as I said in my last two letters, there is simply no use in your sending me any more samples. In the first place, as I've said before, I don't feel that your drawings are right for my series. They are too stark. They would be better suited for science fiction, or mysteries, or books of that nature. They are definitely not for my squirrel series. And, as I have also said before, art samples should be submitted to the publisher, not to me. This is not my decision to make.

"There would be absolutely no point in your coming here to talk about your work. I don't like to be this rude, but your insistence forces me to. I wish you good luck in placing your artwork elsewhere, but please do not keep bothering me with it."

Keith looked at me silently, then slipped the envelope into his pocket. He glanced through the rest of the letters, but nothing about them caught his interest.

I said, "Do you think that artist guy could have been so mad at her rejecting his illustrations that he'd come here and . . . ?"

Keith shrugged. "You wouldn't think so, but you never know. Did you remember where you heard the name before?"

I screwed up my face and tried. "Nope, sorry."

"Well, keep thinking about it and let me know.

I'll check this out from his home address and see what gives."

Aware of the passing of time, I left then, to get Betty's food from the kitchen cupboard and Gruffy's from the basement.

When the animals were taken care of, I walked down the hill toward the shop, muttering to myself, "Richard Moline, Richard Moline."

THREE

Dad met me at the door
of the shop, pulling on his jacket.

"Hold the fort till I get back, will you? They've
got a dead tree fallen across the ten-k loop of
the snowmobile race course, and the first races
start at one. If Harold calls again, tell him I'm
on my way up there with a couple of chain
saws."

He backed the pickup out into the street, and
I turned to face the morning's complications. The
shop was full of people hanging around. Only
four people actually, but in snowmobile suits they
seemed to take up an awful lot of room. Ray

Proctor was there again, and Bernie Rodas and two guys with familiar faces but no names I could remember.

I wasn't in much of a mood to sit around gossiping with this crew, which of course was what they were there for. I kicked off my boots, threw my parka into the corner, and elbowed my way behind the desk.

Bernie came and hovered over me. She hovered a lot, and she had the build to do it with. Her camouflage-colored snowmobile suit was zipped open clear down the front, spilling out an old flannel shirt that showed gray ski underwear at the neck. She was probably no more than twenty-five or so, but looked older with her thick, rough skin and short-cropped, oily hair. She was a practical nurse at the hospital, but she seemed to work very flexible hours, especially when there was snow. She'd bought an old beat-up black and yellow Ski-doo snowmobile from Dad a couple of years ago, and I'd swear she took it to bed with her at night.

"They were saying you found Mrs. Amling," she said, standing too close to my chair. I wanted to push her away, get out from under her.

"Yeah, and I really don't want to talk about it, Bernie, okay?"

Ray Proctor tipped up a can of beer. It was barely nine o'clock, for heaven's sake. "That must have given you quite a jolt, Clarie," he said. "Finding a dead body like that."

"Like what?" I flared. "What do you know about it?"

He smiled a scum-toothed little smile. "Just what everybody else in town knows, honey. Somebody hit the old lady over the head and wiped her out."

"Just get out of here, Ray," I yelled. "Go bother somebody else. I'm sick of looking at you."

He made a face and took another long pull on his beer can. I couldn't push him out, but I could leave myself. Just across the street in Lions Park, the nine ice sculptors were being turned loose on their blocks of ice. Norm Andersen was in charge of the contest and he probably had everything under control, but I could run over there for five minutes anyway, check to be sure all nine entrants were there.

I picked up the clipboard that had Dad's copies of all of the event entries, and flipped through to the page marked "Ice Sculpture Contest." I went through the motions of reading down the list, to look busy and official for Ray and the other bums.

I stood up and moved toward my boots, then froze and looked again at the list. There it was, the fourth name down. Richard Moline.

Dialing Keith's number, I glanced at the four

interested faces watching me. Too late, it occurred to me that maybe I shouldn't be making
this call in front of them. But Keith was already
on the line.

"Hi. It's Clarie. Listen, you remember that
name we were talking about? Moline? He's here,
in the ice sculpture contest. Just thought you
might like to know."

When I hung up, the four faces were avid with
curiosity. "Who was that you called?" one of the
guys asked.

"None of your business. It wasn't anything,
anyhow."

Ray hooted. "That was the Sheriff's office, I
bet. What's Dittmer want to know about a name
for, huh? Got something to do with old lady
Amling?"

"Of course not, stupid." I couldn't think fast
enough to make up something that would sat-
isfy him, so I scuffed into my boots, grabbed my
parka and the clipboard, and ran across the road
to the park.

The park was one square block, and all it held
was a bandstand in the center, and sidewalks
crossing in an X, with beds of cannas and mari-
golds around them in the spring. Big old oaks
dotted the park, and there were a few iron
benches and a flagpole. That was about it.

The nine blocks of ice were set up in a circle

around the bandstand. Each block was four feet high, three feet wide and two feet deep. They'd been made in a rough, tin-lined wooden box near the water fountain, beside the steps up to the bandstand. Water had been piped from the base of the fountain into the form. Each block had taken about ten or twelve hours to freeze solid, so Norm Andersen had been at this project for more than a week, wrestling with frozen water pipes and the job of getting each ice block hauled into place.

The blocks were numbered, one through nine. Richard Moline had drawn the number four block.

I climbed the steps to Norm's headquarters in the bandstand and said to him, "Everything going okay here?"

"No sweat. Everybody got checked in on time, and I started them right at nine. They all know the rules: They can work from nine to five, no later, no earlier, and they have to be done by Saturday afternoon. Nice bunch of people."

He looked slowly around the circle, and so did I. Beside each block was a man or woman studying drawings, etching lines onto the blocks, squinting, studying.

Casually, I hugged my clipboard and began walking around the circle, smiling at the artists if they looked up and smiled at me. Most didn't; they were too intent.

A little way from block number four, I stopped. Richard Moline was short, very short, no more than five foot three or four, I guessed. He was broadly built through the shoulders and had stubby, square little hands. His face was the type that went with scars and broken noses, although it had neither. He was bare-headed, and I could see dead-looking brownish hair, thinning, and red-rimmed ears.

He didn't look like an artist who wanted to illustrate children's books. He didn't look like an artist at all, although he was moving in a businesslike way around his ice-block, scoring cut-lines in it with the corner of his chisel.

Did he look like a murderer?

Yes. Maybe. Possibly.

I found myself staring at the ice chisel and wondering.

Dad sent me home for lunch, and I was glad to go. Rover had stayed home for once, probably because of his house guest. Betty Cocker wrapped herself frantically around my legs, whining her need to be held. I heated a can of spaghetti, stirring it with one hand and holding Betty. Her breathing sounded a little looser today, rattly, like a chest cold breaking up and leaving. And she ate a little spaghetti with me.

It occurred to me that we probably had ourselves a new dog. And probably a goat. I couldn't imagine any heirs showing up to claim either one.

I sat with my feet up on the opposite chair, Betty Cocker in my lap, and hard thoughts chasing through my head.

Somebody had killed Mrs. Amling. Richard Moline, the rejected, frustrated illustrator who, according to Mrs. Amling's letter, drew pictures too stark for children's books, was in town for the ice contest. Could he have decided to go and talk to Mrs. Amling in person while he was here? Maybe she was outside when he got there; she insulted or rejected his artwork, and he hit her. Maybe with his ice chisel? I shuddered.

The shop crowd disappeared after lunch. The first of the snowmobile races started at one in the Zumbrota National Forest, and Ray and Bernie and the others had hauled their machines there for the competition.

Around three, Dad sent me up there with the trophies for the afternoon's four races. I drove our pickup slowly, absorbing the beauty of the place. I never got tired of it. A narrow blacktop road twisted through the forest, following a stream bed, then climbing again to a meadow. The trees were giant white pines that shaded out the undergrowth and carpeted the ground with decades of shed needles. The trees were mounded with snow now, and the stream was just a flatness under the snow.

I passed the turnoff to the scout camp, and another to a public camping area. Finally I pulled up at a log lodge at the edge of a broad meadow. Here the parking area was clogged with cars and pickups, all pulling snowmobile trailers. Roaring engines shattered the air.

I carried the trophies down a slope to the starter's table, where a clot of people stood around talking and watching the starting and finish lines. Timers stood at both lines, sending racers off at timed intervals to disappear down a track into the trees. No one was emerging to cross the finish line, so I guessed the first race was still going on, with snowmobiles strung out all through the hills on the twenty-kilometer track.

Someone shouted, "Yay, here come the trophies. We were worried they weren't going to get here on time."

"Never fear," I said. "My dad knows how to run a winterfest."

"Yeah," someone else yelled, "complete with murder mystery and everything. Hey, Clarie, did Mrs. Amling really get murdered, or was it an accident, or what? There's all kinds of stories flying around."

"Nobody knows for sure," I said shortly. I didn't want Mrs. Amling used this way.

A woman holding a stopwatch at the finish line said, "I heard they picked somebody up for questioning already. Some guy that was entered in the ice sculpture contest. Is that right, Clarie?"

Everyone else looked at me, as though they'd already chewed over this bit of information and just wondered what I'd have to add. I was as surprised as anyone else. Richard Moline, picked up already? Keith really worked fast. I was also surprised at the speed that news got up here, but then I realized people had been driving up from town steadily for the past few hours.

"I don't know anything about that," I said.

"Moline, the guy's name was," said another winter-wrapped figure. It was Ray Proctor. He was looking at me, challenging me with the name, knowing it was me who had called Keith with the information about Richard Moline just a few hours ago.

"I've got to get back," I muttered, and fled to the truck.

Dad and I drove home together at suppertime. There were no new crises at the shop, and it looked at though we'd have a quiet evening at home. I was more than ready for it, and so was Dad. He looked more tense than I ever remembered seeing him.

When we got home I started up the path toward Mrs. Amling's to feed Gruffy, but Dad stopped me. "I'll take care of the goat, Clarie. You go on in and start us some supper. And listen, Babe, lock the door after you, okay?"

I stared at him. He must really be thinking about murderers all of a sudden, with all this locking doors, and offering to do the goat chores. He'd never worried about me before. Neither had I. This wasn't that kind of town. Kids ran around outside after dark all the time, playing games and whooping it up. Nobody worried about them.

I shuddered. But I locked the door behind me, and I didn't relax until Dad was back home again.

We had an easy supper, cans of corned beef hash and lima beans, and defrosted stewed tomatoes from our garden. I was in charge of the garden; in fact, it was my main summer job now that the house was built. I wasn't especially crazy about the weeding part of it, but every time I packed away another plastic bag of green beans or broccoli or asparagus into the freezer I felt like I was making a genuine contribution to the family, and I loved that feeling. Dad was crazy about snowmobiles and bikes, and we both loved our little house and our little town, so that meant we were never going to have much money. Nobody makes money selling snowmobiles in a little town. But Dad was doing what he wanted, and that was the important thing for both of us.

What I'd end up doing I wasn't sure yet. I had

thought about getting a degree in conservation and maybe working with the park commission or at the forest reserve or something like that. Except I didn't want to leave here for the four years it would take to go to college. And studying wasn't my strong point. I did what I had to to get by in school, but I never put much effort into it. My life seemed centered in the woods, with Dad, not around school and school friends. Of course I had friends, Bonnie Crowder and a bunch of others, but I didn't seem to need to be with them all the time, not in the way they seemed to need to be with each other.

We didn't talk much through supper, but we did while we cleaned up the dishes. It's impossible to do dishes with somebody and not talk.

Dad said, "I wouldn't say this to anybody but you, because it sounds heartless and terrible, but I can't help worrying about what this business is going to do to the Fest."

"Mrs. Amling, you mean?"

"Mmm. If it had been just a death, you know, illness or accident, it would have been sad, but it wouldn't have people talking a mile a minute like this situation has, you know? I mean, everybody liked her, but she wasn't from around here, and not many people even knew her all that well. Probably you were closer to her than anybody else in town. But the idea that there might be a murderer loose in Harmon Falls, that scares people."

"Well, naturally," I said. "It scares me."

"Good. You stay scared, and you stay careful. I don't want you anywhere outside this house alone after dark, till they get this thing cleared up, okay?"

"You got it."

"Listen, Babe, are you okay? I mean, you saw something over there that nobody your age ought to have to see."

I hugged him. "I'm fine. You just worry about your Fest."

Around nine, just as we were yawning at each other and debating about staying up for one more television program, Keith came over. I turned off the set and perched on the sofa arm.

"How'd it go?" Dad asked. "Are you holding that Moline guy?"

Keith turned on the stove, shook the coffee pot, and held it under the faucet. "Nah, had to let him go. He knew Mrs. Amling all right. At least he'd been writing to her. And he did go out to her place to see her Wednesday morning. Said he knocked at the front door and nobody answered, so he left. He wouldn't have seen her body—it was around the other side of the house. I think he was probably telling the truth."

He knocked the old coffee grounds into the

garbage bag under the sink and filled the basket with fresh coffee. I went into the kitchen end of the room and got down a box of chocolate chip cookies and put them on the table. The three of us sat around the table comfortably, quietly, old friends in a sad situation.

"How do you know he didn't do it, then?" I asked.

Keith dipped into the cookies. "For one thing, the coroner says she died sometime Tuesday afternoon, and Tuesday afternoon Richard Moline was teaching a class at the Minneapolis Art Center. I checked. He didn't check into the inn till Wednesday afternoon."

"For another thing?" Dad prodded.

The coffee bubbled and settled into a steady perk. Keith glanced at his watch. He liked his coffee perked five minutes exactly.

"For another thing," he said slowly, "Moline is too short. That blow came straight down on top of her head. It had to be from a very tall person."

"There was a slope there," I reminded him. "That bank sloped down toward the basement door pretty sharply."

"Yeah, well, he still couldn't have done it if he was teaching a class in charcoal sketching a hundred miles away from here when she died. Listen, I came by to ask if you guys could take care of her animals till her sister can get here from Colorado. She doesn't seem to have anybody closer."

"Sure," Dad and I said together.

We drank our coffee, dropped cookie crumbs down our fronts, and followed our own silent thoughts.

FOUR

We slept until almost eight the next morning, tension exhaustion probably. We might have slept later except for dogs clawing at us, needing to go out.

I staggered around, pulling on my ski underwear, corduroy jeans, and wool sweater over a warm turtleneck. This was the day school was let out for the Fest, so my friends would be all over the place, driving around from event to event, competing in some. I took a little extra time trying to subdue my hair, just in case I should want to look nice for anyone. My hair was wiry-curly, and it pretty much did what it wanted to. About the only way I could dominate it was to cut it off.

There wasn't anybody I especially wanted to look nice for at this point in my life. In fact I had about decided I was never going to be the boyfriend type. What I had instead of boyfriends were secret crushes, usually on absolutely hopeless people. Old married teachers, sometimes even women teachers. The basketball coach the one year I went out for basketball. That was before I learned one of life's major lessons. Tall is not the same as coordinated. She who towers above her friends is not necessarily born with the ability to aim a ball into a hoop.

And, I don't know, I guess I've never been the rah-rah school spirit type, nor the team-player type. I'd rather go off snowmobiling with Dad or deer hunting in the fall. Neither of us was any good at hitting the targets, so we didn't have to worry about actually killing a deer. But the hunting was exciting, tracking the deer and getting close enough to try a shot.

So, although I feel as though I fit into Harmon Falls very well, I don't exactly fit into the high school gangs and cliques and don't really want to. Some of those girls can be so cruel. I've seen the way they just decide they don't like a certain person, and after that, whatever that person says or does just gets ridiculed. Most of the kids treat me okay, at least to my face, but I'm not stupid. I know they consider me kind of an oddball because of the way Dad and I live. But I think they respect me, too, because they know I don't care all that much whether they freeze me out or not. I can get along without them . . . so they tend to accept me as I am. Bonnie is the only one I'm really close to, and even she and I tend to go our own ways more than best friends usually do. That's probably why my friendship with her has lasted so well: she allows me that freedom.

As I got dressed Friday morning, I couldn't help feeling a little smug in my position as assistant-bigshot of the Fest. While the rest of them might be competing in ski races or snowmobile races, Clarie Forrester was going to be checking, overseeing, and trophy-delivering, and I'd rather be me than them.

In my eagerness to get into the day, I'd almost forgotten Mrs. Amling, until Betty Cocker tripped me up on my way to the kitchen.

Dad was stirring eggs in a skillet. He made great scrambled eggs, with bacon crumbs and onions and parsley and anything else that came to mind.

I sniffed over the skillet and said, "Should I run up and feed Gruffy, or will you snarf up all the scrambled eggs before I get back?"

"Sit and eat. We'll drive over there on our way to the shop."

I poured coffee for us both, plunked the toaster, and glanced at him. "Are you saying you don't want me going over there alone even in daytime?"

"Well." he shrugged. "Give me your plate. Not exactly, but yeah, kind of. We just don't know what kind of mind . . . what kind of person could have done that to Mrs. Amling. I'm not taking any chances with you, Babe."

"Dad, we don't even know for sure that she was murdered. I mean, look, she died from being hit on the head, but we don't actually know that anyone did it. It could have been some kind of accident, a branch blown down from a tree, or something like that. I know, I know"—I held up my hand—"there wasn't any branch lying there, nor anything else that could have done it. So if whatever hit her wasn't there, that must mean somebody took it away, which would mean somebody hit her with it or else why would they take away the whatever, and not call the authorities. Now you've made me do it again."

"What?" He grinned at me and skimmed a piece of toast across the table at me like a Frisbee.

I caught the toast and glowered at him. "You

made me talk myself out of my own argument by not interrupting me."

Everything was quiet at the A-frame. I fed Gruffy, then walked slowly around the house, staring up, down, and all around, trying to think of some way her death could have been an accident. Finally Dad honked and reluctantly I loped to the truck and got in.

"This morning," he said as we coasted down Cardinal, "we've got the dogsled races starting at nine, ski races starting at ten, and then the women's snowmobile races starting at one. And this afternoon the kids will be getting signed up for the mutt races tomorrow. Remind me to have the newspaper photographer out there for the mutt races. That and the dogsled races; they always make good news pictures."

We parked in the alley behind the shop and came in the back way just as Norm Andersen charged up to the front door and banged frantically on it.

"Oh, God," Dad muttered as he fumbled with the lock, "what's gone wrong with the ice sculpture contest?"

Norm burst in, his round face and bald head a startling shade of red. His eyes were bulging.

"Mel, you better get over here right now. This is awful. You're not going to . . . I've never seen anything like it. Call the Sheriff. Clarie, don't you come. You stay here. Call the Sheriff, quick."

"Why? What? What's . . ." But he and Dad were already halfway across the street.

I dialed Keith but it was the dispatcher, Mary, who answered. "Mary, this is Clarie Forrester. Listen, where's Keith? They need him double-quick over at Lions Park, but I don't know what for. Something at the ice sculpture contest. Norm Andersen was just here popping his gaskets and telling me to stay away."

"He'll be there in five minutes." Mary wasted no words.

Hitting the lock on the shop door, I pulled it shut and ran across the street, almost colliding with a van pulling a dog trailer and carrying a dogsled on its roof. The people in the van waved good-naturedly as they swerved to miss me.

Near the bandstand a small crowd had gathered. They seemed to be mostly the sculptors; several had forgotten tools in their hands. They stood in a circle, staring at one of the blocks of ice. I could see Dad's bald-spotted head above the crowd, and he was staring, too, at the ice block.

I hesitated, puzzled. There had been nine ice blocks set, evenly spaced, in a circle around the bandstand, so that each block had plenty of space around it for watchers to stand, and for judges to walk all the way around and view the statues. Last year there had been some genuinely beautiful ice statues, one of a dozing fawn, one of a Scandinavian troll, one I remembered especially: a crouching panther, with every fang detailed, a curling tongue, and glaring eyes.

But this block, which was holding everyone spellbound, wasn't one of the nine that had been here yesterday. It was outside the circle, standing close to the wooden mold in which the blocks were made.

I snaked through the crowd toward Dad, and when I broke free so that I could see the block clearly, I stopped and stared, like everyone else.

This block wasn't silvery-clear as the others had been. This block had colors within it, reds and blues and tan . . . oh, my God.

A face stared out through the ice. A distorted face, its terror literally frozen in place.

As I looked, other details began showing through the glitter and glare of the ice: a hand with fingers splayed, grasping. A knee, bent so that it came close to the surface of the block, so close the fabric of its jeans was clear. The denim was worn through to frayed whitened threads bridging a bare kneecap.

My ears began ringing. Dizzily I tried to look away, but the face drew my eyes. I knew the face, even as distorted as it was by death and by the

ice around it. I'd only seen that face once before, but I knew it.

It was Richard Moline.

My stomach didn't settle down again until I
was half a mile into the Forest Reserve with a
load of dogsled trophies. Dad had gotten me
away from that ice block as soon as he realized
I was there, sending me off in the truck to run
errands and get away from the horror.

But of course, there was no getting away from
it. It wasn't just the death, it was the maniacal
way the man had been murdered. And there was
no question about this one. It had to be murder.
And the worst of it was, no one had any idea
who did it, so some crazy was running around
loose in Harmon Falls. Nobody was safe. Nobody was going to be safe again until the crazy
was caught.

I found myself staring around me at the forest I'd always loved and felt at home in. Now my
imagination flared. Suppose the truck stalled.
Suppose I was stuck out here all alone and the
murderer came along and offered me a lift. I
wouldn't have any idea who it was, whom to trust.
The whole thing was a nightmare.

I pulled up outside the log shelter house
which, this morning, was headquarters for the
dogsled races. Dad had warned me not to talk

about the ice block thing to anyone up here. Two miles from town, maybe no one would have heard about it yet.

But as soon as I started toward the timekeeper's table with my box of trophies, I knew someone had already brought the story. People came toward me, avidly staring, wanting details but hesitating, too, held back by a kind of delicacy. It was as though they were ashamed to show their own eagerness.

I set the carton of trophies on the table and said to Carmen Hoyle, "Here's for today's races. We've got, let's see, Two-Dog Team, One Year and Under; Three-Dog Team, Four-Dog Team, Open Team, Drivers Under Sixteen . . ."

"That was terrible, what happened in town," Carmen said. She was in charge of the dogsled races. She and her husband traveled all over the Midwest racing their dogs. He did the driving, Carmen did all the rest of the work. She was a nice lady, probably fifty or so, with dyed black hair and an obviously fake lip-line painted on.

She said now, "I heard it was one of the ice sculpture contestants. Do they know who did it yet?"

Her husband, looming behind her, said, "Boy, they say dogsledders are a competitive bunch. At least we don't go around stabbing each other in the back and making ice cubes out of the corpses."

"Harvey, shut up," Carmen snapped. "That's a terrible thing to joke about. The poor man."

"Was he stabbed?" I asked. I hadn't intended to be drawn into the topic, but I couldn't help it.

"That's what Jim Frazier was saying," Harvey said. "At least that's what it looked like, from what they could see through the ice. Oops, better get back to work."

A two-dog team pulling a low wicker sled came trotting out of the woods onto the race course. The small red-suited figure on the sled stood and shouted and the dogs broke into a weary lope as they passed under the Finish Line banner. Harvey clicked his stopwatch and wrote something on his clipboard. The driver, a boy of about ten, stepped off the still-moving sled as his parents grabbed the dogs from either side and led them away.

"Good time," the mother said. "You cut a full four minutes off your time at Greenwillow."

The boy pulled his cap off, and turned into a girl. Hard to tell at that age, when they're all wrapped up in winter clothes.

Harvey yelled, "Get your three-dog teams on deck. Johnson, you're up first. That's number thirty-seven. Thirty-seven? Hey, Johnson, you got the wrong number on. Your three-dog team is thirty-seven. There, okay, now are you ready?"

A little distance from the finish line was the starting point, a narrow alley marked off with snow fencing for about ten yards with a starting flag midway along.

Johnson and family dragged their lead dog by the harness, struggling to keep him from biting at their arms, the dog was so keyed up. All three dogs in the team were Siberian Huskies, two silver and one red and cream, all with coldly staring blue eyes and handsome fox-like faces. The lead dog thrashed and kicked his hind leg over the harness.

"Hold on," Johnson called to the starter. "Got to get this idiot straightened out. Okay, let her rip."

Johnson stepped onto the sled and gripped its handles.

The starter stared at her stopwatch, nodding her head in time with the jumps of the second hand.

"Ready," she called, and in unison the watchers along the starting alley chanted, "Five, four, three, two, GO!"

The Siberians lunged into their harnesses and galloped away, almost jerking Johnson off his perch. They disappeared into the woods, following the sled tracks through the snow.

I collected the completed entry lists from Carmen and the envelope of entry checks for today's races, then started reluctantly back up the slope to where the truck was parked. I did not want to go back to town. I wanted to stay up here in this mountain meadow, surrounded by pine forests, where people were having simple fun driving dogsled teams in friendly races.

When I got back to the shop Dad was on the phone and half a dozen people, most of them in snowmobile gear, were standing around talking excitedly.

Dad had his palm over one ear and was yelling into the phone, "Listen, can you talk a little . . . no, nothing is cancelled. Whoever told you that was wrong. The snowman contest will start at ten tomorrow, on schedule. No, there's no reason to . . . no . . ." He hung up, cursing under his breath with words I'd never heard him use before.

He looked up at me and said, "Babe, run over to Keith's office, see if you can find out anything about Moline. I've got to have something to tell these people. Parents are calling in, scared to bring their kids into town for the events tomorrow, and that's half our income from those entry fees. If we have to start refunding just because of this . . ." He slammed his palm down on the desk and stared around him as though he were looking for an escape.

I loped up the block to the building that held the town hall, library, and Keith's office in the back. It was a scuffed, khaki-colored place with posters showing safety tips for handling firearms and reviving choking people.

Mary was the only one there. She sat behind her scarred counter with her bank of radio controls. She was a leathery little woman, tan hair and skin and no makeup of any kind. Her lips had freckles on them. She wore a slightly unraveling reindeer sweater over her police uniform because they had a lot of trouble with the heat in there.

She looked up over the counter at me and didn't smile.

"My dad sent me over to see if you guys have found out anything yet about Mr. Moline. He's . . ."

She raised her hand to stop me as her phone rang. When she got back to me, I went on, "He's trying to reassure people over there, but some of them are beginning to cancel their entries. Everybody's panicking."

"Listen, I'd panic, too, if I had time," she said in her gravelly voice. "We don't know anything yet, the coroner is examining the body over at the hospital. At least, he will be as soon as they get the ice melted. We don't know anything at this time."

"Hey," I said, "this is me, not some reporter trying to pump you. Can't you give us something reassuring that we can tell people?"

Mary's face lightened a shade. Her phone rang again. As she reached for it, she said, "Tell them the investigation is proceeding. What else can we say? Hello, Sheriff's office."

Trudging back toward the shop, I was hailed from a passing car full of kids from school. "Hey, Clarie," somebody yelled, "you hear about the frozen stiff? Isn't that wild?"

From within the car a boy's voice sang, "Leprosy, my God, I've got leprosy. There goes my eyeball, into my highball. . . . tra la la . . ."

I threw my hands into the air and made a motion waving them away. This wasn't something I wanted to make jokes about. It was too awful, for the victims and their families, for everybody in town who might be in danger, and on a lesser but still serious level, for Dad and me. If the Fest folded halfway through, and if the bad memories from this year squelched subsequent Fests, it was very possible that Dad and I might not be able to go on making a living from the shop. So much of the snowmobile business was generated by the Fest races and publicity.

People were being killed here, and possibly a way of life, too. I was relieved when the car full of kids drove away and left me alone.

FIVE

After lunch Dad sent me out again, this time to the campgrounds on the other side of the lake where the cross-country ski races were starting. I offered to stay and hold down the office if he wanted to do the running around, but he said no, and waved me off with another box of trophies. I guess he was so distracted trying to convince people not to cancel their entries and leave town that he'd talked himself into thinking there wasn't any danger in Harmon Falls.

And of course there wasn't any, really, I told myself as I steered the truck down Main Street through the slow-moving traffic and past the concessions trailer at the main intersection of town. No one was going to go around murdering people in broad daylight in the middle of town. Still, I stretched across the cab and plonked down the lock button on the far door, something I'd never done before.

Off the highway at the far edge of town, I followed an arrow-marked gravel road that twisted among acreages and vacation cabins to the lake shore, then followed the shore to the state-owned park and campground. Straight across little Harmon Lake, I could see the line of downtown stores and the bandstand in Lions Park.

In the broad parking circle in front of the shelter house, cars with ski racks on their roofs stood, doors open, while skiers bent to lace their boots or stretched to slip skis out of carrier bags. Just like the dogsled races that morning, this place seemed, on the surface, to be a happy gathering of people bent on enjoying a winter afternoon on their skis.

But underneath . . .

I hefted my trophy carton and approached the center of the activity, a starting line marked by a pair of orange flags on either side of the ski track. The track itself reminded me of inverted railroad rails: a pair of flat-bottomed grooves, ski-width and four inches deep, eight inches apart, packed into a broad semi-leveled swath made by the track-laying machine dragged behind one of our snowmobiles.

Several skiers were standing or shuffling in a rough line behind the starting flags. At thirty-second intervals, one of them would move into position for the countdown and send-off, regulated by two high school girls with clipboards and stopwatches. They were the Brinkman sisters who were dead-serious skiers themselves and would be competing in tomorrow's longer races. Today's races were just short warm-ups, three kilometers and ten kilometers.

When the last of the ten-k racers had been counted off and had disappeared from sight around the bend and into the woods, Bev Brinkman came over to me. She took the trophies and said, "I was hoping your Dad would bring these out. I need to talk to him."

"You and the rest of the town. He's up to his belly button in people wanting to cancel entries."

Bev was a sharp-featured blond, who would have had no color in her face at all if it hadn't been for the black mascara and eyeliner. She was a hard-voiced, competitive type, and I'd always avoided her around school, when I could.

"Well, look," she said, "you tell your father we're going to have real problems out here if he doesn't start taking my advice. We've got diagonal-striders competing in these races against skate-skiers, and of course they're getting creamed. You can't hope to diagonal-stride against a field of skate-skiers. I told your father last year, and I told him again this year, you have to have separate divisions, freestyle and skate only, or freestyle and diagonal only. These people are really getting steamed."

I tightened my jaw. Such a stupid thing to be hassling about, with people being murdered in town. Diagonal-striding was the old traditional style of skiing, arm swinging forward with the opposite leg, like walking. Skate-skiing was a newer, faster style, like speed-skating on ice.

"Bev, Dad told you, on trails like this there's no way of policing a whole ten-k course to keep people from skate-skiing. Any skater who wanted to could enter a diagonal only race and start skate-skiing as soon as he was out of sight of the race officials. And that would cause more hard feelings than having open races. Now, I'm sorry, but there's nothing we can do about it. You'll just have to make people understand. Where're your entry lists?"

She pulled the lists from her clipboard and handed them to me, blowing a strand of hair away from her face.

"I guess you're right," she muttered. "Everybody's a little edgy today."

I grinned. "That's okay. It's kind of nice to have something else to argue about, besides . . . what's going on in town."

"What is going on? I heard about the guy in the ice block. God, how awful. Was he frozen to death, or what?"

"Stabbed, they think. Probably dumped in the ice form afterwards, and then taken out early this morning, after he'd . . ."

She met my eyes and shuddered. "Well, all I can say is, let's hope he was already dead. Can you imagine how that would feel?"

"No, and I don't want to. Listen, Bev, are people out here cancelling or talking about it?"

"No, well, we had two cancellations in the ten-k and one in the three, but that's about par for the course. Mostly people are just talking about how corned-up the snow is getting and which wax to use for it."

From the starting flag, her sister called, "Bev, come on. We've got to get these three-k's started."

Hurriedly I said, "Try to keep people's minds off the murders, will you? Thanks."

She motioned me away with her hand and yelled, "Okay, you three-k-ers, line up in any order you want to go, stay toward the back if you're not too fast so you won't lose time stepping aside for the faster skiers. Remember, you follow the green trail markers, not the red ones. Got that? The green trail markers, and you'll circle to the right, go around the edge of the hayfield, back into the woods, down a ravine, back up and to the right again, and back along the lake shore. You can't get lost if you follow the green markers. Okay, first up? You going first? Okay, five, four, three . . ."

I left them to it and went back to the truck, but sat for a few minutes with my arms across the wheel, chin on knuckles.

I wanted my world back the way it was two days ago. I wanted the biggest problems in my life to be Bev Brinkman and her skate-skiers. I wanted it to be last week again, when Mrs. Amling was fixing hot spiced Dr. Pepper for me and stewing about illustrators for her squirrel book; when my life stretched unruffled before me. Our winterfests would grow more popular every year, Dad and I could go on forever making a livable profit from the shop. Now everything was soured. Mrs. Amling was horribly gone from my life, and the Fest was threatened. The Fest and our futures, Dad's and mine.

The gravel road took me back to the highway, but instead of turning right and heading back to the shop, I went straight across the highway onto what was now the north end of Cardinal Road. I wasn't quite ready to give up the peace and beauty of the countryside for the madness of the shop, so I decided I'd stop by Mrs. Amling's and feed Gruffy, stop home and let Rover and Betty Cocker out for a quick potty run, and maybe make some sandwiches to take back to the shop.

The road dipped into the creek valley and followed the snow-blanketed creek around three gentle bends. I braked when I saw three does poised beside the road. They stared at me, gauging my speed and distance, then bounded across the road, sailed over the wire fence, and slowed to nibble sheared cornstalks. What a great world it would be, I thought, if it wasn't for the people.

I could see Keith's cherry-top parked in front of the A-frame before I turned in. I pulled up beside it, did the goat chores, then went in through the basement door and up into the kitchen.

"Keith? Can I come in?"

"If your nose is clean."

At least he could still joke. That was something. He was slouched in the chair at Mrs. Amling's desk, leafing through a book manuscript.

"How come you're here?" I asked him. "I figured you'd be out chasing down leads about Mr. Moline."

"What do you think I am doing?"

I dropped my parka on a chair and stretched out on the brown sofa. So many winter afternoons I'd spent here when Mrs. Amling was finished with her day's writing and felt like company. My throat hardened painfully as I thought about the loss of her.

I said, "You think the same guy killed both of them?"

He grunted and leaned as far back as the desk chair would carry him. "Well, that's a possibility. But."

"But?"

"But. There's another possibility—that Moline was killed because somebody was under the impression that he had killed Mrs. Amling."

"But he didn't. You said you had to release him after you questioned him, because you checked him out and found out he couldn't have killed her since he was teaching a class in Minneapolis at the time."

He held up one finger. "That's true. But. A lot of people in this town know I took him in for questioning. But when I turned him loose a few hours later, who knew he'd been cleared? Mary had already left for the night. I drove Moline back to the park and left him there to pick up his tools and car. Then I came straight out to your place. By this morning the whole town would have known he'd been cleared, but between nine and midnight last night, which was when he was murdered, nobody around town knew that."

I pondered. "But if that was why Mr. Moline was killed, that would mean that somebody completely different killed Mrs. Amling. It wasn't Moline and it wouldn't have been Moline's killer, because then he wouldn't have had any reason to kill Moline, not if he knew he'd killed Mrs. A. himself."

"I know it," Keith growled, "and that's what I can't figure out. This town hasn't had a murder in sixty years, and then it was a battered wife killing her husband. It's too much coincidence to think these two murders aren't connected in some way. But, damn it, where are the motives for either one of them?"

I lay staring at the high, planked slope of the ceiling. "What about Ray Proctor? Could he have killed Mrs. Amling, do you think? I mean, it seems a little far out that he'd kill her just for firing him last summer, but I always did think he was about half a bubble off plumb anyway, and people have done stranger things."

Keith shook his head. "It's possible. He was driving a stock truck for the sale barn Tuesday morning, but he didn't get there till about ten, and he lives alone so there's no way to prove when he left home. Still, I don't think so. I mean,

I've known Ray all his life. He's as lazy as a warthog, but I can't see him doing anything as vicious as . . ." He motioned toward the window below which Mrs. Amling had died.

I sat up and leaned against the back of the sofa, stretching my arms out along its length. "Well, what about Mr. Moline? Did you come up with anybody who would have any other reason to kill him?"

Again Keith shook his head. "Nah. I checked with his ex-wife, which was as close to a relative as I could find. She said he was a loser, but not the kind to make enemies. She's happily remarried, it was a no-contest divorce several years ago, and she said he's not successful enough as an artist to create any professional jealousy. He's entered ice sculpture contests before, at winter carnivals and such, never been better than third or fourth place, so it's a sure bet he wasn't knocked off by a competitor."

We followed our silent thoughts for a few minutes; then I said, "So what are you doing out here again? What are you looking for?"

"Damned if I know. But if Moline was killed out of revenge by someone who mistakenly thought Moline had killed Mrs. Amling, then whoever that person was, he had a pretty strong emotional connection with the woman. You don't kill to avenge the death of a casual acquaintance."

"So could it have been Ray? I mean, maybe when he was working for her last summer he fell madly in love with her and that was really why she fired him and why he went around telling everybody she had the hots for him. Like wishful thinking and saving face at the same time. Do you think so?"

He shrugged. "Again, possible, because Ray said he was home alone last night, and there's no way to prove it or disprove it. But still, I don't think so. I don't know. It just doesn't seem logical."

He stood up and began working his way around the room, picking up standing picture frames and sliding out the pictures.

"What are you doing that for?" I asked, and went to join him. Because the walls sloped, most of the pictures stood on tabletops and along the back of the desk rather than hung on the walls. They all seemed to be of her husband and of women friends, probably other authors.

"Just looking. You can help if you want. Sometimes people slip new pictures over old ones in a frame. See if you can find any of anyone here in town, or anything at all that doesn't strike you just right."

I slipped a few dead-husband portraits out of their frames and found nothing behind them. On the stereo in the corner were a clutter of smaller frames holding snapshots. I looked at each but nothing rang a bell until, behind one of them, I found an older snapshot.

It was in black and white, a man, woman and child standing on the steps of a vacation cabin. The woman was a younger Mrs. Amling, probably in her early thirties, with a slimmer face and long, blowing hair. But it was definitely her. The man was her husband, the same square face and low hairline as in twenty other pictures around the room. He wore shorts and a Hawaiian shirt and held a canoe paddle in one hand.

The little boy between them was square-faced, too, his face wrinkled and squinted against the sun. He wore jeans and a T-shirt over a stocky body.

A family portrait, apparently. And yet Mrs. Amling had never been able to bear children, and had never mentioned a child, adopted, foster, or any other kind.

I tilted the snapshot toward the window light, and stared hard at the boy's face. There was something about it . . . almost familiar, but camouflaged by the child's youth, by his squint, and by the fuzziness of the camera focus.

I gave it to Keith.

"If there was a child . . ." he said, staring as I had stared at the picture.

"Well, if there was, she sure never mentioned him."

He slipped the picture into his shirt pocket and said, "Let's go through the file cabinets. Look for any personal correspondence, family, friends, anything that might help."

"Can't you just ask her sister?" I asked, moving to stand in front of one of the file cabinets beside the desk.

"I told you, she's on a Caribbean cruise. I won't be able to get hold of her till Sunday, and who knows what kind of state this town will be in by then. And there aren't any other relatives. Mary's been on the phone all day in her spare time trying to find anybody who could shed some light on Mrs. Amling's background. Called her publisher, her agent, her apartment manager where she lived before she moved here. Zilch. The woman really was a loner."

For nearly an hour we went through the two file cabinets, file by file, page by page. There were old book contracts, reams of reviews of her books, old income tax forms.

At the back of one of the drawers Keith dug up a stationery box and opened it.

"Finally," he grunted. The box was full of letters, some from her sister, yielding nothing.

Some were old ones, letters of condolence at the death of her husband.

"Whoa," Keith said. "Listen to this one. 'Dear Mama.' " We looked at each other. " 'Dear Mama, Why did you send me to this place? I hate it here. I hate you for letting them take me here. If you don't let me come home and live with you again. . .' " Keith paused, squinting at the paper. I looked over his shoulder. It was printed in pencil on lined paper torn from a spiral notebook. And yet the printing was somehow adult. There was no date on the letter, but the paper was clear white, probably no more than a few years old at most. And the snapshot must have been fifteen or twenty years old.

I read. " '. . . and live with you again, I will kill myself, and I will kill you, too. You have to love me. Please, Mama, pretty please with cream and sugar on it.' "

"Whew," I said, looking at Keith.

He met my eyes, and nodded, and folded the letter away in his pocket.

"That could be it," he said.

"But it wasn't signed. How are you going to find out who wrote it?"

"Beats the hell out of me, Clarie. Listen, you better get back down to the shop. Your dad's going to be worrying about you. And listen, you shouldn't have been up here, and I shouldn't have been letting you help with a police investigation. Right?"

I nodded. "My lip is zipped. I can tell Dad, though, can't I?"

"Oh, sure, but that's as far as any of this goes till we get it cleared up. Promise."

"Yo."

Before I left, I took another long look at the snapshot. That square face, that bulging forehead. Who did that remind me of? Somebody, somebody I'd seen recently . . .

SIX

As I left the A-frame and got into our pickup, I had a prickly sensation of being watched. I locked both doors and turned on the ignition, then looked slowly around. Hills, trees, the road below, and an open hayfield beyond it, woods again, and full circle to the A-frame, where Keith's figure showed surrealistically through the glare of sunset against glass.

He was watching me, waving me away. But that wasn't where the prickly sensation came from.

It came from my imagination, I told myself firmly as I wheeled the truck around and coasted down the lane toward the road. It came from knowing that I was on the verge of recognizing the face in the photograph, and therefore on the verge of being able to name the possible killer. But of course nobody knew that but me and Keith.

Keith? Square face, about the right age. I shuddered. Nah, not good old Keith. He was Dad's buddy, my lifelong friend. I rejected the possibility totally, but the fact that I had thought about it, even for half a minute, disturbed me. Were trust and loyalty so thin?

There was a car behind me, staying well back. The road dust hid the details from my view, and of course there was no reason why there shouldn't be a car on Cardinal Road at five o'clock on a Friday afternoon. Still, I changed my mind about going home and starting supper in our solitary house. Instead, I coasted down the hill to the shop.

Dad was alone for once and ready to lock up. He didn't say he was relieved to see me, but I could read it in his face and in the lightness of his movements as he pulled on his jacket, un-plugged the coffeepot, and locked the front door.

"I want to drive around and check things before we go home," Dad said as we climbed into the truck.

"Oh. I guess I was hogging the truck all afternoon. Sorry about that."

"No problem, I couldn't have gotten away anyhow. How were things at the ski races?"

I'd forgotten all about that, what with the business out at Mrs. Amling's. "It was okay, no more cancellations than usual, Bev said. In fact the main topic of conversation out there seemed to be keeping the skate-skiers and the diagonal-striders off each other's necks."

We drove out through the Forest Reserve to check on the snowmobile races, which had just finished for the day. Only two cancellations in that department: Bernie Rodas, who had been entered in the women's twenty-k, and Marge Smith, also in the twenty-k, who had had car trouble and hadn't gotten there on time.

Driving back through the blackening forest, Dad said, "Funny, Bernie would cancel. She's been looking forward to that race for months."

We turned off onto the lake road and stopped at the ski race headquarters, but everyone had gone. One last check, at the ice sculpture area, then on home.

Rover was in a tear to get outdoors. He'd been left in the house to keep Betty Cocker company, but he was not an indoor type and he let me know it by racing furiously away into the woods as soon as the door was open. Betty looked from me to him, hesitated a minute, then raced after Rover.

After supper we tried to settle in to television

watching, but the wind had risen, and on windy nights the antenna didn't work too well. The picture was snowy, so we turned it off and pulled our chairs closer to the wood stove, in winter talking position with our feet on the stove's fenders.

I got up when I thought I heard the dogs at the door, but it was only the wind. Our house wasn't usually drafty, but in a strong west wind like tonight, I could feel the air move.

I settled into my chair again and wrapped my sock-covered toes around the stove fender. In the silence, I thought about the photograph, the letter. I'd told Dad about them earlier while we were driving around.

The room was very quiet. Outside the wind whooshed through the trees; in here there was only the snapping of the firewood and the distant sound of Rover barking. The barking came down the chimney in an eerie way, as outside sounds always did in the winter, when doors and windows were double-sealed.

"Squirrels on the roof," Dad said.

I listened. There was a creaking of roof timber, a light scratching. Wind and squirrels. Yes, sure. What else would it be?

"You scared?" Dad said suddenly, shooting me a slanted look.

"Yeah, a little bit. Aren't you?"

"Yeah, a little. Don't think there's any reason to be though, not really."

I nodded in forced agreement.

"Still," he said, "I don't think I want you tagging around after Keith while he's working on this. I don't want you involved in it, period. There is obviously a screwball in this town somewhere, and a damned dangerous one. I don't want whoever it is to get the idea you could be a threat to him in any way. Got me?"

I nodded.

"Okay then, it's low-profile time, Babe. And I think we'd better tell Keith to get somebody else to take care of the goat for the time being. I don't want you going over there for any reason, even in daylight. They think Mrs. Amling was killed in the daytime, and that is a very hidden house over there. Nobody going by on the road could see much of what was happening back around the buildings."

"Fine with me," I said, more than a little relieved.

I slouched over on one elbow and tapped my teeth with my fingernail. "If only I could think who that little boy in the picture looked like. Dad . . ."

"Yo."

"Did you know Keith when he was little?"

He looked at me strangely. "Where did that question come from?"

"I know it's a stupid idea, but did you?"

He frowned, crossed one foot over his knee and squeezed his stockinged foot, bending the toes back and forth thoughtfully. "I think he was about, I guess, junior high when he moved here. I seem to remember being on the junior high track team with him. Or no, that was Joe Harms I'm thinking of. I can't honestly remember when I first knew Keith. High school anyway. I know he lived here all through high school, because that was when we were running traplines all winter before school, trying to save up for motorcycles."

"Could he have been adopted, do you think?"

He bent his toes back till they popped. Again the sound of the dogs barking in the distance came down through the stovepipe.

"Nah, I wouldn't think so. He looks more or less like his folks and nobody ever said anything about him being adopted. If he'd been the kid in the picture, he'd have to have been adopted by his present folks at a pretty old age, ten or so anyhow. He'd have talked to me about that, I know."

"And besides," I added, "even if he had been Mrs. Amling's former adopted child, or whatever, and had some sick attachment to her all these years, that would have been too much co-incidence for her to move to a little place like Harmon Falls, where he just happened to be liv-ing."

"And," Dad added, "he wouldn't have killed that Moline guy. He wouldn't have had any rea-son to. Besides the fact that he's my buddy, he's a good man and he wouldn't do these things. He just wouldn't."

"I know it," I sighed. "I don't know what got me onto that kick. I was just trying to think of anybody I knew who had that square kind of face and who would be around the right age."

"Well, if Keith is right about the second mur-der being revenge for the first one, what that means is two dangerous people running around loose, not just one. I hate this whole thing, Babe. And I especially hate it coming right now, during the Fest."

"Yeah." To change the subject, I asked, "Want to play some Yahtze?"

We played in an absentminded way for a cou-ple of hours till the dogs came home and we could all go to bed.

The next morning while I was starting break-fast, I turned on the television to see what the morning news had to say about the Harmon Falls killings. But the picture was unwatchable and even the sound was bad.

"That damned antenna," Dad muttered. As we left the house, he turned and looked up toward the roof, then stopped and grabbed my arm.

The television antenna was definitely bent out of shape, but that wasn't what we stared at. A path of packed snow led from the corner of the nearly flat roof up to the center, where the stovepipe rose. The path was about as wide as a person's body, a person crawling up to lie beside the stovepipe chimney.

At the corner where the track began stood our firewood stack, three or four feet high on this end, and stairstepped. An easy climb for anyone who wanted to listen in . . . anyone who couldn't hear through the double windows but who knew sound traveled down stovepipes. And up them.

We stared at each other, remembering what we'd been talking about when we heard squirrels on the roof. I'd been saying I could almost place the face in the snapshot.

Oh, God.

That morning, Dad took over the errand-running, figuring I'd be as safe in the shop as anywhere. He drove off a little after nine to deliver trophies and settle problems at the peewee ski on the other side of the lake and to swing around by the dogsled races which, this morning, were kids-only races. This was Saturday, and most of the activities were for little kids.

At ten, Reverend Hyslip stuck his head in the shop door and said, "Clarie, is your dad around? They need him over at the mutt races."

"He's out at the peewee ski. I don't know when he'll be back. What's up?"

"They need somebody over there to take charge of the mutt races. Bernie Rodas was supposed to be doing it, but she hasn't shown up yet, and some of the mothers are getting antsy. Can you get somebody to take care of it?"

I stared at him, dismayed. "How about you?" I asked hopefully.

"Sorry, kiddo. They've got me judging the snowman contest and I'm supposed to be over there right now. Somebody just hailed me as I was going past the mutt races and asked me to send help."

"Oh, that's right. I knew we had you down to judge something or other. Okay," I sighed. "I guess I'd better lock up here and go do it myself."

Reverend Hyslip walked up the street with me, taking my elbow in his nice, old-fashioned, gentlemanly way even though we didn't go to his church, or to any church for that matter.

"I wonder what's up with Bernie?" I said. "She didn't show up yesterday either at the snowmobile race she was entered in. I hope she's not sick or something. . . ."

We stopped walking and looked at each other. Not another murder. Not another victim. Not Bernie. I wasn't crazy about her, but still . . .

I turned and ran back to the shop with Reverend Hyslip right behind me. Bernie lived alone in a little apartment above the dime store. If she doesn't answer the phone, I thought as I listened to it ring, I'll go over there and see.

But she answered. Her voice sounded thick with sleep. "You're supposed to be running the mutt races right now, five minutes ago," I yelled at her. After an instant of relief that she hadn't been murdered, I was furious with her for screwing up the schedule.

She apologized in a disconnected sort of way and promised to get down there as soon as she could. I waved Reverend Hyslip away, and he trotted across the street to assume his duties as snowman judge. I could see the activity over there, small clots of children and attendant parents rolling up snowman bodies. Behind them, the ice sculptures were taking their final shapes; at least eight of them were. Mr. Moline's stood roughly angled, unfinished.

Sighing, I locked the shop again and ran up

the block, across the street, and down the slope to the edge of the lake, where several children stood around, holding their dogs' collars. The dogs were mostly large breeds or mixtures of breeds, and they were harnessed to ordinary children's sleds by cheap leather harnesses or homemade rigs of rope or leather straps.

"Sorry about the delay," I called. "Okay, let's get started. First heat is, let's see, Matlock, Jensen, and Breyer? That right?"

I'd brought my clipboard with the master lists of all the event entries. Luckily, the mutt races were simple heat events needing no stopwatches.

Three children of about ten or twelve, two girls and a boy, came forward leading their hitched dogs.

"Okay, you guys, bring them down here. Pit crews?"

Three parents stepped forward to hold the dogs' collars as I lined them up on the ice at the edge of the lake. The racecourse was a straightaway, a hundred yards of snow-cleared ice leading out from the shore toward the middle of the lake. The dogs were pretty much unsteerable once they started running, so the racecourse had to be a straight one, marked only by the clearing of the snow. That meant that the finish line was a hundred yards away.

"I need two volunteers," I bellowed, and three or four fathers moved toward me, looking helpful.

"Listen, I'll start them off from this end, if you guys will go down to the other end and call the finishes. Here, take these, set them about twenty feet apart for the finish line."

I motioned toward the two orange traffic cones left there yesterday for this purpose. We all waited while the group of fathers trudged to the far end of the racecourse, set their finish-line cones in place, then waved.

"Okay," I said to the three waiting racers. The kids lay belly-down on their sleds and got death-grips on the sled handles. The three moms stared tensely at me while they held the dogs' collars.

"Okay, everybody in position? Ready, set, GO!"

The dogs lunged, the sleds bounced across the ice, and the drivers' shrill calls split the air.

One dog slowed abruptly, was rear-ended by his sled, and tumbled backward onto his child. They tipped over and slid several yards to stop in the snow. Another dog veered to the side, spilled his driver, and took off across the lake. The third dog, a smallish setter, ran fast and true and won the heat. I marked the winner on my sheet, and called the second trio of runners into place.

Bernie appeared while one of the mothers was

still struggling to get dog and harness untangled. She reached for my clipboard, muttering, "Sorry. My alarm didn't go off."

Her hair was obviously uncombed, and there was yellow sleep crust in her eyelashes. I handed her the entry list with a feeling of disgust.

"What happened to you yesterday, Bernie? How come you didn't run in your race?"

"I didn't feel too good. Thought I was coming down with flu or something."

"Oh. Are you okay now?"

"Yeah, I'm okay. I think maybe all that about Mrs. Amling kind of got to me."

She really did look pasty. I wondered suddenly if she was afraid. She lived alone and she was kind of an isolated type, now that I thought about it. She never seemed to pal around with the other nurses from the hospital. And the snowmobilers in town, who centered their social circle around Dad and the shop, accepted her in a teasing way, but talked rudely about her when she wasn't there.

For the first time, I felt sorry for Bernie, and painfully grateful to Dad for giving me a place in this town and an identity. He was liked, so I was liked and accepted. If I'd had to do it alone like Bernie, moving into a strange town as she had a couple of years ago, not knowing anyone, wouldn't I be a shut-out, too? I was a little odd in my own way, not hanging out with the kids from school very much, preferring Dad and the woods. How would this town have accepted me, if it hadn't been for Dad?

I patted her padded arm and said, "Well, here you go. This is the second heat, or rather the second trio in the first heat. Jensen won the first run. You know how to do this, don't you? You did it last year?"

"Yeah, no problem. Clarie?"

I'd started away, but turned back.

"Did they find out anything more this morning about that Moline guy?"

I shook my head. "Not that I know of. Listen, Bernie, try to keep people off the subject around here if you can, will you? The whole thing is making people very nervous, especially these parents." I motioned toward the ring of people at the edge of the ice.

She nodded, turned her broad back to me, and bellowed the names of the next three runners.

SEVEN

As the afternoon
passed, Dad's tension gradually lifted. There were
some cancelled entries and a lot of uneasiness
in the crowd, but not the mass panic he'd been
afraid of. Still, we stayed together as much as
possible.

Reverend Hyslip and I were the judges for the
silly sled races on the slope leading down to the
lake edge where the mutt races had been run
that morning. The sleds could be anything but
real sleds: snow shovels, plastic trash bags, garbage can lids. There was a fender from a fifty-
seven Chevy, and the chassis from an old tele-

vision set, and one small child used a toilet lid. The big winner of the day was an old kitchen sink whose driver got her rear jammed in and had to be pulled out of it.

Again today, Dad locked up the shop and simply did business out of his truck, carrying all of the day's trophies and clipboards and records with us, and trusting that anybody who needed him desperately would manage to find him.

At the end of the afternoon we made the rounds again, from the just-ended ice sculpture contest to the snowmobile race area to the finale of the ski races. When we'd finished the wrap-up tour and locked the day's receipts away in the shop, we went home to clean up.

The entry money that the Fest took in was more than swallowed up by expenses, trophies, newspaper ads, and the printing and mailing of flyers, plus the building and maintaining of the necessary equipment such as the ski track-laying machine and the ice-block mold. So it wasn't that Dad and I made any money directly from the Fest. In fact, we donated, along with the other town merchants, to cover the expenses. Our profit came from the surge of snowmobile sales that always followed the Fest from people watching the races. And quite a few snowmobile customers turned into bike customers in summer. So the Fest was well worth our efforts, and by Saturday afternoon it was beginning to look as though even murder wasn't going to ruin this one.

So we went home feeling good . . . until we saw Keith's cherry-top parked in front of our house. Then we remembered the snow track on the roof.

Keith was just lowering himself off the roof via the woodpile as we parked and got out.

"Find anything?" Dad called.

"Nothing usable." Keith landed with a grunt and came into the house behind us, brushing his hands together. "I was hoping for maybe a snag of fabric, or a measurable footprint, but . . . zip. He must have walked in from the road on your tire tracks, where the snow is packed too hard to print. There were a few prints from the tracks over to the house, but they'd been swiped over, probably on his way out again. He bent hell out of your antenna, by the way."

Dad waved that aside. What was a television antenna compared to the chilling reality of a murderer on our roof, listening to me saying I could almost remember who he was? Suddenly the pleasure of the afternoon evaporated.

Keith looked at the coffeepot. I filled it and turned on the stove, then fed the dogs and let them out. "Did you feed the goat?" I asked Keith.

"Yes, but I'm going to be awfully glad when that sister gets here, so she can get rid of the damned thing. I've got a double murder investigation on my hands here. I don't have time to feed some stupid goat every day. And"—he pointed a finger at me—"don't you go over there. Either one of you. It's too dangerous. In fact, I think I'll call the Rooses and see if they'll take the goat. They've got a bunch of them out at their place; one more won't hurt them."

I glanced at the clock. Just twenty minutes till starting time for the chili supper and dance. I went into my room and changed into clean jeans and a blue checked blouse with a big red sweater over it. They were good colors with my dark hair and I knew I looked nice—not that anyone would notice, but just in case.

When I came back into the kitchen Keith was sipping at his too-hot coffee and looking at me thoughtfully. Dad had gone to change, too, so Keith bellowed, "And another thing, I'd feel a whole lot better if you two would stay someplace else tonight, maybe for a few nights till we get this thing wound up. If that guy got up on your roof, he can get into your house. These windows of yours are not exactly maximum security. Heck, some of them don't even lock, as I recall from when you built the place. No offense to your carpentry, buddy, but this is no place to feel safe at the moment. And if this guy has zeroed in on you, or you "—he shot me a look—"to the point of climbing your roof to hear what you're talking about, then I'd be a little worried if I were you."

Dad emerged, sucking in his stomach to tuck in his shirt. He was in his Western stuff, pearl-buttoned tan shirt and brown Western-cut pants and his dumb-looking string tie with the turquoise clasp.

He shot me a look and I gave him a shrug, leaving the decision to him. But I was relieved when he said, "We could probably bunk in with Hal and Joanne for a couple of nights. Pack us some stuff, will you, Babe? We'll just go on over there from the dance. And we'd better get our tails in gear. They're supposed to start serving about now."

I yelled for the dogs. They appeared right away and trotted inside happily enough. Betty Cocker seemed to be having a good influence on Rover. While Dad fed them and stood between their dishes so Rover didn't snarf up Betty's food, I stuffed toothbrushes, shaving stuff and clean underwear into a shopping bag. Then the three of us left together, carefully locking the house.

Back in its early years, Harmon Falls had been a thriving little river port with a fair amount of money coming in from the shipping of lumber from the pine forests around the lake. One of the half-dozen original downtown buildings still standing from those glory days was a square brick opera house at the opposite end of Main Street from our shop. It was small by today's standards, but it was a handsome building, well kept by the town council. There were ornate wrought-iron railings curving out from the upper windows and a landscaped miniature park in the empty lot beside it. Four times a year the community theater put on plays there: *Charlie's Aunt* or *South Pacific* or some such. In between, the basement was used for weddings, dances, the town Halloween party, and the winterfest chili supper and dance.

When we got there, the room was full of people standing around, most of them still in their outdoor clothes. Several skiers padded around in wool socks and ski underwear bottoms below their turtlenecks and sweaters. Children's voices were shrill above the general talk and their small bodies chased and darted through the room. Committee women had rolled out lengths of cheap white paper for tablecloths, cutting it at the ends of the long tables and taping it down.

At the far end of the room, near the windows opening into the kitchen, two more long tables held the vats of chili, trays of bread and crackers, pans of salads and stacks of dense, rich brownies.

Dad and I separated after we'd loaded our

plates, me to sit with Bonnie and some kids from school, him to settle beside Hal and Joanne and inform them of their new houseguests.

Hal and Dad used to have a sideline together, cutting, hauling, and selling firewood, back when we couldn't quite live off the shop. Hal was trying to get his own business going then, too, doing custom Caterpillar and road-grading jobs.

They gave up the firewood business after Hal got his Caterpillar paid off, because it was too much work for the money. But they were still good buddies and went snowmobiling together a lot on winter nights. Whenever Joanne wanted to go with them, I usually baby-sat her kids, or sometimes we'd all go, kids and all, if it wasn't too cold a night. Those were great times. Joanne was a lot of fun, and there was always an electric kind of excitement about being out at night with a full moon lighting up the whole world and the roar of the engines between our legs. It was great when Dad and I went alone, but when the bunch of us went together, I'd get a kind of bursting feeling in my chest as I roared over a hump, yelling and laughing. It was a feeling of "This is it. Life is never going to get any better than this moment." And I'd know that this instant was burning itself into my memory, to be savored fifty years from now, when I was an old lady.

It felt good to settle in beside Bonnie at the long, paper-covered table. She was much smaller than me and had a kind of pixie look to her that matched her sense of humor. I can't remember when we started gravitating toward each other, some time around fifth grade, I think. She had a rare quality of accepting everyone just as he or she was, even an oddball like me.

"How did you do in your three-k?" I asked, blowing on my chili. She was a plodding skier, but good-natured about it, and she'd entered the 3-kilometer race just for the sake of being involved.

"Finished twelfth," she beamed.

"Out of?"

"Fourteen. You had to ask, didn't you? Oh well, if God had meant me to be a jock, she'd have given me longer legs. How have things been going with you? I've just caught fleeting glimpses of you whooshing around town in your truck."

I shrugged. Bonnie's face darkened. "Say, I was really sorry to hear about Mrs. Amling. You really loved her, didn't you?" she said.

I looked at her, surprised that she'd known that. She flushed, embarrassed, and gripped my knee as a substitute for the hug we couldn't quite exchange in front of the whole town.

When everyone had finished eating, we all ganged up on the tables, stripping away their paper coverings, tipping them on their sides and folding up their legs, then stacking them against the wall. A very loud Western band from Zumbrota set up their amplifiers and instruments and webs of wiring in the far end of the room, and the dance was on.

They started with polkas. Dad came and found me and away we went, foot-stomping, arm-pumping, whirling, and colliding with other arm-pumpers. We were good. We were damned good, and I loved dancing with him. He was the only partner I'd ever had who could actually keep up with me. I pulled in at his side and, arms around waists, eyes on the floor in front of us, we shuffle-stepped in a giant circle, with other couples falling in with us. By the end of the Too-Fat Polka, we were puffing and sweating but ready for another round.

After a few warm-up polkas, the band went into some Willie Nelson, and Dad and I split up. He stooped over poor little Joanne, who is only about five feet tall, and bent her back out of shape dancing her through "Blue Eyes Crying In the Rain." I danced a couple with Bonnie, since we both felt like dancing and the boys didn't know enough to appreciate us. Then the band went into some hard rock and everybody just danced en masse.

The evening passed, and I could feel no difference in the mood of the crowd this year from other years when the Fest wasn't marred by murder. If people were upset about Mrs. Amling and Richard Moline, they were setting those feelings aside for the evening.

At least there was a feeling of safety here in this crowded basement room with practically the whole town and a bunch of Fest visitors all packed in together. Whatever evil there was in this town, it was outside somewhere, and it couldn't hurt any of us in here.

Ray Proctor grabbed my wrist and pulled me out onto the dance floor for a slow dance. There was no one I'd less rather slow dance with, but it didn't seem worth the effort to hassle with him. I just tried not to let him pull me in too close. He had a stale sweat smell to him.

"So what's new with your buddy the Sheriff?" he asked, blasting me with yucky breath.

"What do you mean?"

"You know. He caught the murderer yet?" His eyes glittered at me, as though he was talking about sex, not murder. Maybe the two gave him the same kind of kick. My hand went clammy in his. I studied his face as casually as I could, but, much as I wanted it to, it just didn't fit the square, bulge-browed face of the child in the snapshot.

"Why ask me?" I snapped.

"Oh, you and your dad just seem to be awful

buddy-buddy with old Dittmer. I just figured you might know something the rest of us don't."

He backed me into someone. When I turned around to apologize, it was Bernie Rodas dancing in a straight-arm hold with one of the snowmobilers from out of town. From the look of fierce determination on her face, I guessed she probably asked him to dance or picked him up and dragged him bodily.

"Well?" Ray demanded, trying to pull me in closer to his beer belly.

"Don't ask me, Ray. I don't know a thing about it."

"Well, from what I hear, Dittmer thinks whoever killed that ice carver wasn't the same one as killed Hope."

"Hope?" I was startled, hearing him use her first name. As close as I was to Mrs. A, I'd never called her that myself. Something about her, some shy dignity, seemed to forbid it.

"Mrs. Amling, rather. Dittmer thinks the ice carver guy got bumped off because somebody thought he killed Hope, even though he didn't, and wanted to get back at him. And I heard you and Dittmer found some picture or something, some kid of Hope's, who Dittmer thought might be living in town here."

I stiffened. If Ray knew about that, anybody in town might. I looked around at the dancers close to us, looked for a man with a square face and a bulging brow who might be listening, might be looking at me and deciding I was dangerous to him.

"I don't know anything about any picture, Ray, and would you keep your big feet off mine? I'm going to be crippled by the time this incredibly long song gets over with."

Near midnight, Keith appeared at the edge of the dance floor, out of uniform and drinking a plastic cup of coffee. He had a vague smile on his face, covering a distracted expression. I left Bonnie and went over to him.

"Anything new?" I asked under the blare of the music.

"Nothing good. Talked to Moline's girlfriend. She said about the same thing the ex-wife had said, Moline was basically a loser with no enemies or friends, really. I asked her how he happened to contact Mrs. Amling in the first place, and she said he just sent out samples of his art to six or seven children's authors around the Midwest, hoping some of them would like his stuff and put in a plug for him with their publishers. He wasn't all that good, apparently, and all the authors brushed him off. There wasn't anything special about Mrs. Amling, except that she lived in Harmon Falls, and he decided he'd pursue her while he was in town for the Fest."

"So she didn't think anybody from up there would have any reason to kill him?"

Keith sighed. "Right, and I checked her alibi, hers and the ex-wife's both. No hope there. So that brings it back to a revenge thing, and that leaves me with two separate murders done by two different people. God, I wish I'd gone to computer school like my mom wanted me to."

Moving closer, I murmured, "Ray Proctor was just asking me about the investigation like he thought I had inside information or something. And he said it's all around town about me finding the snapshot and letter."

"I know it. I tried to keep it quiet, but in a town like this . . ." He waved his coffee cup helplessly. "I'll just say what I said before, Clarie: I want you and your Dad to stick together every minute of the day and night till this is over, and I don't want you spending the nights at your place. Hear?"

I nodded. "We'll be at Hal and Joanne's. With all their kids, I won't even be alone in the bathroom."

"Good. Don't take any chances. If anything happened to you . . ."

"Don't worry, it won't," I assured him. And wished desperately that I believed myself.

EIGHT

Sunday morning, the final day of the Fest. I sat on the tailgate of our truck, my back against the door rim of its fiberglass top. Behind me were the cartons holding today's trophies, and odds and ends of tools and junk.

Before me spread the mountain meadow at the top of the Forest Reserve, with the shelter to my left, and parked dogsledders' rigs on either side. Down the slope was the starter's table, the starting and finish lines, race officials with clipboards and stopwatches, and clusters of people, dogs, and wicker sleds.

Dad was down there, talking and joking and giving a good imitation of a man with no worries and a good night's sleep behind him. I was fighting a headache myself from sitting up talking at Hal and Joanne's till three in the morning, and then having to sleep with their two littlest boys, at least one of whom is a bed-wetter. He didn't actually get me during the few hours I slept on the edge of his bed, but the thought of the possibility had made it hard to drop off to sleep. That, and everything else.

This morning, all that was going on was the wind-up of the dogsled races up here and the grand finale thirty-kilometer ski race down at the lake. This afternoon would be the final snowmobile races, up here after the dogsledders were finished. So there was a bigger crowd watching the dog races than there would otherwise have been. Most of the snowmobilers were here, waiting around for their turn on the course after the dogs.

The day was starting out bright and warm, with lots of unzipped jackets and glistening melting snow. The sun was bright, the sky a cloudless blue.

With all my heart I wished that this were an ordinary Sunday and I were watching ordinary dogsled races in this beautiful place with all these nice people.

All these nice people, and one or two vicious murderers. I hugged myself and glanced around to see if Keith might be here. He wasn't.

Restless with my apprehension, I slid off the tailgate and wandered down the slope just as Dad was coming up. He muttered an oath under his breath.

"What's up?" I asked.

"First dogsled team just got in," he growled. "Said there's another dead tree across the trail. He had to go clear off through the brush to get around it. I told him we'd give him another run."

He went past me to the truck and reached in for the chain saw he always carried in there. "Okay," he bellowed to the crowd, "who wants to mush me out to the upper loop?"

A man with a five-dog team waved him over and they drove off together, laughing. I saw Dad brandishing the chain saw over his head, and a sudden frightening tremor shot through me, as though I were seeing him for the last time.

The families attached to the waiting dogsled teams began milling impatiently, knowing their races would be delayed a good half hour or more. Some began unhitching their dogs. One little girl, just in front of me, wandered off, pouting and complaining about her cold ears. She was the one I'd mistaken for a boy at the first races on Friday. I smiled a little to myself, thinking how unisex children of that age can look, especially with short hair and jeans and no gender-shape to their bodies yet.

The smile hardened on my face.

How similar boys and girls of that age can look . . .

My mind raced. A whole new area of possibility opened up in my head. Suddenly something clicked. My eyes widened, and into their range came the face I'd been looking for so frantically. A broad, square face with a bulging brow. A familiar face.

The figure stood just a few yards down the slope from me. Our eyes met, and my horror was reflected in the gaze that met mine. Horror, and recognition.

Instinctively I spun and raced for the truck. Keys in the ignition. Ignore the bouncing tailgate. I had to get to Keith.

As I roared out of the parking area and onto the downward winding road, it occurred to me that it might have been better to wait till Dad got back from the tree-removal. But my instincts cried, get away from there! Get to Keith. He's the only one who can protect you.

I drove crazily. I hadn't been driving long enough to have a sure feel for high-speed turns, and it was sheer luck that I got down to the bottom of the wooded valley without meeting a car coming up. On either side of the road, dense green pines towered, striping the snow with blue shadows and dropping soft loads of melting snow. But I didn't see the trees, only the charcoal ribbon of blacktop in front of me and the banked snow along its edges.

When I could flash a glance at the rearview mirror, I thought I saw a car or a truck, or something colorlessly dark behind me, too distant to be definite.

"Hold on," I told myself grimly. All I needed now was to run off the road and give the car behind me a chance to catch up. Out here in the middle of the Forest Reserve, I could be well and truly bashed to death before anyone happened along to stop it.

Across the bridge, hard turn to the left and onto the level stretch that followed the creek. Looking left, I could see across the creek to the road I'd just descended . . . and the car was there. Heart racing, I stomped on the gas pedal and hung onto the wheel for dear life. Literally.

I climbed up out of the woods. Past the stone entrance gates to the Reserve, a skidding left turn onto the highway, and blessed beautiful Main Street. Keith's car wasn't in front of the town hall, but then he often parked in back.

I slammed out of the truck and ran inside. Mary wasn't on duty on weekends. At her desk sat a young man whose name I didn't know, a rookie deputy of some kind.

"Where's Keith?" I demanded, breathless.

"He's out of the office, but he should be calling in at any . . ."

"Where is he? I need him right now. Emergency!"

He stood up. "Can I help?"

I was almost crying with frustration, and it didn't occur to me that he was an officer and probably could help. I wanted Keith! "No," I yelled. "Where is he?"

"Out at Mrs. Amling's, I think. He said something about stopping out there to do something about a goat, and then he was going . . ."

But I'd already slammed out. As I darted for the truck I looked both ways. The street was empty. The car wasn't there.

Safety was at Mrs. Amling's, then. I peeled away from the curb, narrowly missing the car parked in front of me, and wheeled around the corner for Cardinal Road.

Our house looked peaceful as I drove by.

I turned in at Mrs. Amling's, even though I could see that Keith's car wasn't there. Leaving the truck running, I made a dash for Gruffy's pen.

The little goat greeted me with bleats of hunger and loneliness. His feed pen was empty, and so was his water bucket. Keith hadn't been here yet.

I hesitated, thinking I'd better get back down to the Sheriff's office where there was at least the protection of the young deputy. But as I turned, a car came into the lane and stopped there, blocking my escape.

Panic froze me as Bernie Rodas ambled toward me, her broad face unsmiling.

NINE

My body was rigid with fear, but suddenly my mind started working. I couldn't get away in the truck, even if I could get around Bernie, because her car blocked the lane and the ditch dropped off too steeply to drive around her car and get back onto the road.

She was between me and the truck, and she was also between me and the path through the woods to my house. I might be able to outrun her, but on the other hand she was insane, probably with maniacal power that my fear-weakened legs might not be able to match. And in the woods, Keith wouldn't see us if he drove in, which he could do any minute, if I could just stay alive long enough. The woods behind me were a dense tangle of gooseberry bushes and saplings. I knew better than to try to get through there.

That left the house, which was on my right, midway between Bernie and me. The sloping bank where Mrs. Amling had died was right there, and so was the basement door, which might or might not be unlocked. If it was, I could get in, lock it, and call for help on the phone.

Trying not to show my thoughts, I began walking as casually as possible toward the house.

"Hi, Bernie. What are you doing here?"

Her eyes riveted mine. "I can come here if I want. This is my mother's house. Did you know that?"

I was at the corner of the house. Forcing one foot after the other ahead of me and keeping my eyes on Bernie, I said, "Your mother? I didn't know that, no. Was she?"

"You know she was. You saw a picture of her and me and her husband."

"Well, I saw a picture," I said in a voice that quavered slightly. I backed up until my hand was on the doorknob. Turned it.

Locked.

Bernie came closer.

Suddenly there was a flash of movement beside my face, a cold whoosh.

I screamed. Bernie jumped.

Stuck in the snow two feet to my left was a mammoth icicle nearly a yard long and as thick as my arm.

I looked up. High above me rose the triangled dormer end of the A-frame, the glass wall of the living room rising almost thirty feet above my head as I stood in the downhill depression outside the basement door.

Hanging from the peak of the eaves was a row of similar icicles, formed by the melting of sunny days and the freezing of the nights, and all on the verge of breaking loose in this morning's sun.

Swooping fast, I picked up the fallen blade of ice. Even with its narrow bottom point broken off in the fall, it was still well over two feet long, and heavy.

I held it in front of me as a lion tamer might hold a chair. The answers were flooding into my mind now on a charge of adrenaline.

"Here it is," I said almost gently to Bernie. "Here's what killed Mrs. Amling. Remember, we had a big snowfall, lots of ice, and then a couple of days of warm weather just before she died? Remember, Bernie?"

She stared at me, uncomprehending.

"She was killed by a falling icicle, Bernie. She must have come out the basement door just as it fell, and it pierced her skull. Something this big and sharp, falling from that high . . . and then by the time we found her, the icicle had melted away. Those two days were so warm last week."

She took another step toward me, shoulders hunched, fingers splaying ominously.

I raised the icicle. Its cold was numbing my bare hands, its surface turning to water in my grip.

"You killed that man for nothing, Bernie. He didn't do it. She died from an accident."

She met my gaze then, and from the deep hollows of her eyes I saw a despair so black it stopped my breath.

Into the silence that hung between us came a car engine, a slamming door, a shout.

She turned toward the shout. In her camouflage snowmobile suit with the pouch of its hood riding her shoulders, with her arms still outstretched, fingers splayed, she looked like a bear, a cornered grizzly, outnumbered but still dangerous.

I raised the icicle overhead, ready to swing.

Keith came at a run, with Dad close behind.

"Grab her, she did it," I yelled.

Bernie lunged past them, making for her car,

but Keith brought her down with a football tackle and Dad piled on top. She bellowed, an inhuman sound I will never forget, and she fought them with startling strength. I ran in with my icicle at the ready, but Keith was no amateur at this. When he rolled off her, her wrists had been gathered into handcuffs. He and Dad had to lift her to her feet by her shoulders.

Dad came to me then, held my arms and stared at my face as though he'd never expected to see it again. "Are you all right?"

My voice didn't work, but I managed a nod. I was coming unglued now, shaking legs, churning stomach, buzzing in my ears.

We started down the lawn toward the cars, but suddenly I stopped.

"Keith. The house keys."

"What?"

"Throw me the keys to the house. Nobody fed Gruffy this morning."

Dad laughed and cried then, and hugged me till my ribs cracked. Together we fed the goat, then followed Keith's car downtown.

TEN

That night, after the last of the Fest activities had been wrapped up and the town was ours again, Dad and I and Hal and Joanne hauled our snowmobiles up to a big hayfield above Cardinal Road and just roared our brains out. We'd done the same thing other years, just for the relief of having the Fest over with and being able to ride ourselves, instead of supervising everybody else.

This year, for Dad and me anyhow, it was the best way in the world to blow away the tension we'd been living under. To celebrate. Hal and Joanne were full of questions about what happened with Bernie, but Dad said to shut up and ride, we'd talk about it later. I think he really needed to get some space and some clear night air between him and the scare he'd had.

I didn't have my own snowmobile so I used an old Polaris trade-in we had down in the shop. It was big and noisy and stiff handling, but that was fine with me. I needed to burn off my overload of adrenaline, just like Dad.

Joanne had left the kids with her mom, so it was just the four of us adults tonight. The moon was just past full, and with the reflection from the snow, the world was light enough to see details. We turned off our headlights and ran side by side over the hayfield, roaring up out of the dips and sailing airborne from the rises.

At the far end of the field, we turned our lights on and went single file across the downed stretch of fence and into the woods beyond. We'd run in here a lot. The guy who owned the land was a buddy of Dad's. In fact these were the woods where Dad and Hal had done most of their firewood cutting years ago, so we all knew our way.

Going single file and slower now, I had a sensation of being carried along, being surrounded by loving friends: Dad behind me, Hal and Joanne in front. I felt as though, even though I was running my own machine and could get into trouble, nothing bad could happen to me with these people around me. It was a strange but lovely sensation after what I'd been through.

Out of the woods again, a few fast swoops around the hayfield, then, in wordless agreement, we pulled up in a loose line at the high point in the hayfield and cut off our motors. From here, there was a sharp cutbank down toward Fox Creek. Across the creek was Cardinal Road, and beyond the road, the land rose again, wooded on that side. Through the trees I could just see the glittering reflection of the glass triangle of Mrs. Amling's A-frame. Beyond that, hidden from sight, was our own unique little house.

Now that we weren't racing through the air, it felt warm against my face. I pulled off my parka hood and gloves, and rested my feet against the dash. Talking time had come, I knew.

Joanne said, "Okay, Mel, enough is enough. If you've never seen a person die of suppressed curiosity, open your eyes, buddy. It could happen any second."

Dad laughed and flung his arms in a broad stretch. "Well, like I told you before, it was Bernie Rodas that killed that Moline guy, because she thought he'd killed Mrs. Amling, but he hadn't. It was a freak accident with an icicle. Once Clarie figured out that it must have been a falling icicle, the police lab double-checked and verified it. Who would have thought? I mean, do I have a smart kid here, or don't I?"

"Yes, I know, but what happened? Why? What, when, where, who and all the rest of it?"

Hal said, "Shut up and let him tell it."

I could see Dad was going to keep teasing them, so I jumped in. "What happened was, I'd seen that snapshot, and that weird letter someone had written Mrs. Amling. I kept trying to think who the little kid might be, but for some reason I was assuming it was a little boy. I don't know, it just looked like a boy. You know how kids that age can fool you sometimes if you don't know them? Especially this one, in jeans and T-shirt, and with, I don't know, heavy-looking features. And scowling or squinting in the sun, it just looked like a little boy. But it wasn't. There was this little girl at the dogsled races that I'd mistaken for a boy when I first saw her. And this morning I saw her again, and that started me thinking, what if it was a little girl in the snapshot instead of a little boy? And right away, it just clicked in my mind, and I knew it was Bernie Rodas. And she was standing right there, watching me figure it all out. She could tell, the way I looked at her . . ."

"And like a fool," Dad said, "Clarie panicked and took off, instead of waiting for me to get back from the trail. When I got back and found out she'd taken off, I panicked myself and made Ed Johnson drive me into town. I ran into Keith and told him what happened, and he and I took off looking for her." He gave me a long, warm look.

I said, "Bernie followed me back to town, and right out to Mrs. Amling's. If I'd had half a brain I would have stayed right at Keith's office till he showed up."

"But if you'd done that," Joanne said, "probably no one would have figured out what did kill Mrs. Amling. If you ask me, you are the big hero of the day."

I shrugged and grinned.

Hal said, "So what was Bernie, Mrs. Amling's daughter, or what?"

Dad jumped in then. I knew he couldn't resist telling. "Keith finally got a call from Mrs. Amling's sister just after he'd arrested Bernie, and she filled in the other part of the story."

Joanne demanded, "Yes, but what was Bernie? You're the most aggravating storyteller I ever knew."

I got into the act again. "What the sister told Keith was that Mrs. Amling and her husband had taken a foster child, years ago, because she couldn't have children of her own. It was this little girl named Bernadette, who was about seven or eight and had already been in some pretty serious trouble. Her mother kept having kids by different fathers, but she didn't take care of them or hold them or talk to them or anything like that. Bernadette seemed to have no sense of right or wrong. She could lie or steal or hit other children with no conscience at all.

"So I guess the authorities advised the Amlings to try a foster-care situation for a few years before they made up their minds to adopt her. They figured she just plain had a criminal mentality and it wasn't going to get any better at that point, even with loving care."

Dad butted in and took over. "Well, they had her for about three or four years, and then the husband died. It was officially considered an accident—he was under his car and it slipped off the jack and killed him. But Mrs. Amling and her sister both had their doubts. The sister told Keith that the little girl was so fanatically possessive of Mrs. Amling that she was jealous of the husband and was building up a real hatred toward him. So after he died, of course Mrs. Amling didn't feel that she could keep the little girl. She sent Bernadette back to the state, and the kid went through several years of correctional homes and reformatories."

I said, "She kept writing these begging letters to Mrs. Amling. Mrs. A told her sister about the letters. And Bernadette—Bernie—would come around whenever she wasn't locked up someplace and hound Mrs. A. That was why Mrs. Amling moved here, trying to dodge Bernie."

Joanne said, "So that was why Bernie moved here, too, huh?"

"Yes," I said, "but apparently Bernie had simmered down by that time. She still had this worship-thing for Mrs. Amling, but I guess by the time she came here, she had it more under control. She didn't actually bother Mrs. Amling here. At least I don't think she did. I never saw her over there. She must have been just sort of worshipping from afar."

"Until," Hal said.

"Right. Until." I shuddered. "Until she jumped to the wrong conclusion about poor old Mr. Moline after Keith took him in for questioning. She just went bonkers, didn't wait to make sure he'd really done it. She was following when Keith took Mr. Moline back to Lions Park to pick up his car after the questioning. From what Bernie told Keith this afternoon, she just followed Moline over to the ice sculptures, and when he started gathering his tools, she . . ."

I didn't like to think about that part of it, but Hal was able to fill in. "Stabbed him with his chisel, dumped him in the ice block mold, turned the water on, and filled it up around him."

Joanne said, "God, she must have waited around for hours while that block froze, and then hauled it out and set it up by herself. That took strength."

"That took insanity," Dad said. "Just think of all the sorrow that could have been avoided if only someone had loved that little baby."

We looked at each other, and I knew what he was thinking. He was remembering when I was a four-pound preemie baby in an incubator, with a sixteen-year-old mother who had panicked and fled rather than face the responsibility of me.

He was thinking, and I was thinking, too, what might I have turned into if he had abandoned me?

Beyond the darkness of Cardinal Road, I could just see the lights along the highway. There to the right was Keith's office with its one cell holding Bernadette Rodas.

Dad and I looked at each other. We didn't smile, but it was all there in our eyes, the acknowledgment of our great good fortune.